The Women's Club

The Women's Club

Vanessa Davies

LIBRIS

An *X Libris* Book

First published by X Libris in 1995

Copyright © Vanessa Davies 1995

The moral right of the author has been asserted.

A CIP catalogue for this book
is available from the British Library.

ISBN 0 7515 1343 1

Photoset in North Wales by
Derek Doyle & Associates, Mold, Clwyd
Printed and bound in Great Britain by
Clays Ltd, St Ives plc

X Libris
A Division of
Little, Brown and Company (UK)
Brettenham House
Lancaster Place
London WC2E 7EN

The Women's Club

Chapter One

JULIA MARQUIS WAS smiling to herself as she parked her BMW in the car park of *Sybarites*, the exclusive Women's Health Club which she now owned outright. It had been part of the divorce settlement that she should be allowed total ownership and control of the business she had worked so hard to build up. Inevitably her husband Leo had been too busy with his other pet businesses to pay much attention to their joint venture, while she had sweated blood to get it off the ground, so she regarded it as her moral right to claim it for her own.

Now Julia took a keen pride in every detail as she walked through the swing doors into the lobby. It had the feel of a high-class hotel about it, with relaxing sea-green décor, deep leather armchairs and an atmosphere that bore just a hint of soothing ylang ylang. Behind the attractively scalloped desk and flanked by exotic plants Steven, the receptionist, raised his blond-capped head to smile a greeting at his boss.

'Everything running smoothly, Steven?' Julia enquired, confident that it would be or, if there was a problem, it was being sorted even as they spoke.

She hired only the highest calibre staff now that *Sybarites* had been transformed from a thriving but ordinary health club to the very special establishment it was today.

'Yes, Miss Julia. I've fixed another interview for Warren's job – tomorrow afternoon, it's in your diary. Oh, and there have been two new applications for membership. You're seeing a Rebecca Maitland at eleven this morning, and a Doreen Cadstock this afternoon at three.'

Julia looked first thoughtful, then wickedly amused.

'Cadstock? Not the wife of our esteemed MP, by any chance?'

'The very same,' Steven grinned back.

Once Julia was safely in her office she gave out a giggle of triumph. Well, *Sybarites* was certainly coming up in the world! She glanced through the two application forms which Steven had given her. Rebecca had been nominated by Lou Marsh, so she was probably a model too. They never had much time for self-indulgence, poor things, always jetting off to some remote palm-fringed beach.

More interesting was the fact that Doreen's sponsor was Tanya Wentworth, a woman Julia had always suspected of being Jeremy Cadstock's mistress! Not that any hint of gossip would ever escape the hallowed walls of the Health Club, of course. Members and staff alike had been warned that the law of discretion was absolute, as far as she was concerned. Instant dismissal or a lifelong membership ban awaited any who dared break that rule, and since *Sybarites* was fast gaining a reputation as the smartest place in town, no one who cared about their status in the community would want to pay that penalty.

Promptly at eleven, Rebecca Maitland arrived for

interview. She had the lean, sculpted body that was currently fashionable, and a nondescript face with regular features that Julia knew were selling points, easily transformed into anything the admen thought would push their client's product.

'Come in, Rebecca,' she smiled, offering her hand. 'I'm Julia Marquis, manager of *Sybarites*. I like to interview all prospective members personally, to make sure you know exactly what kind of services we offer here. Has Lou spoken to you about us at all?'

This was a test of Lou's discretion. Rebecca gave only a slight smile, her blue-grey eyes giving nothing away.

'She said it was a really nice place, good for relaxing. I'm a model, like her, so I need somewhere I can retreat to, a place where people aren't coming up to me all the time saying things like "Didn't I see you on the front of *Elle* last month?" Privacy is something I'm prepared to pay for.'

'Of course, and we guarantee absolute discretion here. But we also offer a range of services that other Health Clubs don't. Perhaps you would like to take a look at our brochure?'

Julia handed her a glossy booklet and waited while she flicked through it. The first half described the Gym, Pool, Healthfood Bar, Sunbed, Sauna and Steam Suite. There was also the Spa Treatment Suite, with various seaweed, mud and mineral baths, then the Beauty and Hairdressing Salon. The photographs showed stylishly appointed rooms with all the latest equipment combined with tasteful décor and luxurious comfort. Everything, in fact, that a busy career girl or housewife could desire to keep her feeling young, beautiful and pampered.

Rebecca had reached the massage section, with its detailed description of various techniques and the fees for each. Julia watched her face intently. Suddenly those long lashes blinked and a startled look came into her eyes, which she kept riveted to the page, to hide her confusion. She slowly uncrossed and re-crossed her long legs, coughed, then glanced up, her cheeks pink.

'You're surprised by our intimate massage service,' Julia stated matter-of-factly, saving Rebecca the embarrassment of mentioning it herself. 'Not all our members take advantage of it, of course, but many do and are completely satisfied. There are very strict rules regulating both parties. The masseur is obliged to wear his modesty pouch at all times, and may only use his hands and mouth. Any club member who takes advantage of her masseur in any way, or suggests anything outside the prescribed range of activities, would have her membership instantly cancelled. I hope you understand that I can't risk ruining the club's reputation. If I upset the authorities I might lose my licence.'

Rebecca's reply came out nervously eager. 'Yes, yes, I understand.'

'So, whether you decide to take advantage of this service or not, I must insist on absolute secrecy. I'm afraid I can't let you keep that brochure, for security reasons, but a full tariff is displayed in all the changing rooms, or you can ask to see it at Reception at any time. Were you thinking of using any of our facilities today?'

Rebecca nodded. 'Yes. I have all day free, but I'm off on a shoot tomorrow.'

'Good. Shall we just settle the business, then? There's this one form to fill in . . .'

Once the formalities were completed Julia directed the new member back to Steven, who would make her appointments with the various instructors and therapists and issue her with a bathrobe and towels. Once they had worked out, however, many women preferred to dispense with their robe and spend the whole time in the nude, since the ambient temperature was that of a tropical island. Even the chairs in the Healthfood Bar had warm, furry seats.

Ten minutes later Julia called up Rebecca's schedule on her computer screen. She skimmed through the gym session, kelp bath, swim and sauna until she reached the massage booking. Four-thirty, with Marlon. Good. She should have finished interviewing Doreen Cadstock by then.

The politician's wife was half an hour late, making Julia nervous. She swanned in with no apology and Julia felt obliged to point out that she had a busy diary.

'I'm sorry to have to mention it, Mrs Cadstock, but if you are more than ten minutes late for an appointment with any of our therapists I'm afraid you won't be seen. Most of them are fully booked all day, you see.'

'Quite. Today I was unavoidably detained,' she replied huffily, plonking her large handbag on Julia's desk. 'And I don't have much time now, so I'd appreciate it if you'd sign me in quickly, or whatever you have to do.'

As Julia went into her spiel about the club and its facilities, her misgivings about admitting this supercilious woman as a member grew. She was at liberty to refuse anyone membership without giving a reason. Yet she couldn't afford to antagonise such a prominent local citizen. If she were pleased with the way she was treated at *Sybarites*, Doreen Cadstock would no doubt recommend the place to her influential friends.

'Has Tanya Wentworth told you about our

massage service at all?' Julia asked, impassively.

Doreen's peach-tinted cheeks seemed to grow a shade deeper. She leaned forward, her faded blue eyes showing a hint of fire. Julia suspected that Tanya had been dropping hints, if not revealing all.

'Only that your masseurs are very expert at their job, and leave a woman feeling wonderfully relaxed. I understand they are all male?'

'Yes, like the rest of my employees. I find that our members prefer to be handled by men. And the special service offered by our masseurs is particularly appreciated. Would you care to see our brochure?'

From the way that the woman turned eagerly through the pages until she came to the intimate massage section, Julia knew she was right. Tanya *had* been talking. Yet she had no proof and, in this case, a reprimand would be inappropriate. She couldn't afford to alienate two of the most powerful females in town. Even so, a veiled caution seemed appropriate.

'As far as our staff are concerned, absolute discretion is guaranteed at all times, of course. And we expect as much from our members.'

Doreen Cadstock looked Julia straight in the eye. 'Naturally. I dare say you wouldn't want this place to be classed as some sort of brothel.'

Julia flinched. 'This is primarily a health club, Mrs Cadstock, as you can see from the range of facilities we offer. The optional extra of an intimate massage is a special extension of the normal service, and one which busy women greatly appreciate. After all, a businessman can arrange for a visiting masseuse to give him hand relief, or even full-scale sex, but there is no such readily available option for women. We aim to provide sensual fulfilment and full relaxation in an atmosphere which is tasteful and discreet.

6

And, judging from the feedback, we have succeeded.'

'I'm sure you have, Miss Marquis. And you've reassured me, too. I just wanted to make sure there was nothing sleazy about the goings-on here.'

Julia went on to describe the rules and regulations. Then, once Doreen had signed up and handed over her subscription cheque, she said casually, 'Tanya Wentworth is in today, I believe. Will you be joining her? I could look up her schedule and tell you where to find her, if you like.'

For a second a steely glint showed in Doreen's eyes. 'Oh no, don't bother. I can't stay today. I have another appointment. I lead a busy life, Miss Marquis, so I shall only be availing myself of your club's facilities occasionally.'

'Very well.' Julia rose to open the door. As she went she remarked, casually, I had no idea you and Tanya knew each other.'

'We are old schoolfriends,' Doreen replied, with a touch of frost, as she swept out.

One day, thought Julia with a smile, I might write my memoirs!

She had almost forgotten Rebecca's session with Marlon. Hastily fumbling for her key, Julia let herself into the small room of her office which housed the security video screens. Only Steven knew that she had visual access to every room in the club, including the massage suite, and she trusted him absolutely.

Switching on the channel dedicated to Marlon's massage room, Julia found work already in progress. Marlon, tanned and muscled with his hair falling in dark ringlets, was operating on Rebecca's thin back, kneading and stroking it by turns. She watched his hand drift down to the model girl's buttocks, pinching up the flesh – what there was of

7

it – and working his oiled thumbs insidiously between. Rebecca squirmed a little on the padded table and Julia guessed that she was becoming aroused.

She wasn't the only one. Julia loved watching new women being initiated into the delights of intimate massage by Marlon, Warren, Erroll, Rudolph, Clark or Sylvester. Named after Hollywood sex idols, every masseur performed his job to perfection. They knew exactly how to take a woman from a state of nervous apprehension through relaxation to arousal and satisfaction by slow degrees, so that at no time did she feel pressured or uneasy. They made the whole process seem like the most natural thing in the world – which, of course, it was.

Marlon's hands were smoothing their way down Rebecca's thighs now, moving on to her calves and then back up to brush the outer lips of her sex with delicate fingertips. Unbidden she shifted her legs a fraction further apart, allowing him easier access, and Julia knew the girl was well past the inhibited stage now. She felt her own labia swell and moisten beneath the lace-trimmed cotton of her gusset.

Typically, Marlon refused the tacit invitation to play with his client's pussy from behind, concentrating instead on making long sweeps up and down her legs. He knew that the longer he drew out the titillation the more intense his client's climax would be. Julia enjoyed the sight of his firmly clenched buttocks as he worked, and admired the honed perfection of his musculature. Inside its protective pouch, however, his penis lay flaccid. For Marlon, like most of the other masseurs, was gay and didn't get in the least aroused by the women he serviced. If she could have employed all homosexuals Julia would have preferred it, as a safeguard against indiscretions, but most preferred to work in gay establishments where the pleasure was mutual.

Now Rebecca was having her feet massaged with peppermint oil and surreptitiously rubbing her mons against the soft padding at the same time. Julia guessed she was longing to turn over and have Marlon make free with her erogenous zones. All in good time. Many a woman had discovered that a toe can be as erotic an organ as any other when expertly stimulated.

Julia felt her own toes tingle in sympathy, and a warmth spread through her groin. She envied her clients but, apart from offering herself as a test subject during the selection of new staff, she had never taken regular intimate massages herself. It would be unethical to put herself, literally, in the hands of any of her employees. For one thing, it would make the others jealous, and she didn't want to encourage rivalry. For another, she was afraid it would undermine her authority. She was sure there would always be an aura of arrogance around a man who had frequently caressed her private parts with his hands or mouth, a subtle lack of respect in his manner that might spread like a contagion. No, each prospective masseur had one chance, and one chance only, to show her personally what they could do, and after that they dealt solely with their clients.

At last Marlon whispered, in his rich baritone, the words Rebecca must have been longing to hear. 'Please turn over now, Miss Maitland. I should like to massage the front areas.'

He began by standing behind her head, smoothing across her forehead with his thumbs, gently kneading her pale cheeks, pinching along her jawbone. Julia surveyed the girl's naked contours with interest. Rebecca's breasts lay flat against her

9

chest, their small nipples hard as pink beads, and her pelvic girdle resembled an inverted basin above the bulb-like pubis. Yet her arms were sculpted and shapely, as were her legs. They, of course, would be the parts of her body most on show. The rest was just a glorified clothes hanger. Overall, the combination of boyish slenderness with slight profiling of the muscles was androgynous in its effect. Almost enough to turn a gay man on, Julia thought with a smile, although Marlon showed no signs of being so affected.

Marlon was massaging Rebecca's neck with light upward strokes of alternate hands. She lay with her thighs loosely apart and her breasts rising and falling quite fast. Was she fantasising, anticipating the more exquisite pleasures to come? He was still standing behind her, unseen, as he changed to a downward smoothing of her upper chest. The palms of his hands just brushed her erect nipples as he ended each stroke. And every time Rebecca's pelvis lifted slightly, in a reflex gesture.

Julia could almost feel the girl's relief when Marlon changed to direct massage of her breasts. Rebecca sighed, wiggling her hips voluptuously, as his large hands encircled their contours giving each nipple a light pinching between finger and thumb. She watched the small breasts fill out and lift upwards, yearning for the stimulation to both continue and intensify. After a while, however, Marlon continued one-handed, freeing his right hand to caress the flat plane of her stomach. He paused, briefly, to anoint his palm with a different oil, one that was more aphrodisiac in its effect, then his right hand moved lower towards the cowry-shaped mons. A little mild probing was enough to encourage her thighs to move wide apart, then he came to stand at her side.

Now Marlon brought his lips into play. While his fingers moved up to tease Rebecca's nipples with the titillating oil, he began to kiss her lower abdomen, flicking his tongue due into her tight crevice from time to time until it was opened up to him. Then he plunged his tongue right in and got to work on her labia. He licked up and down her grooves, making sure she was well lubricated with saliva and her own juices, before going on to concentrate more on the clitoris, encouraging it to swell and stand free of its protective hood. One hand came down to stroke her thighs as he licked and sucked, making her gasp with the sudden acceleration of her desire. Then, while his tongue flicked back and forth over the source of her keenest sensation, his finger inched its way slowly inside her, waggling around to make sure that she was wet enough before proceeding further.

Suddenly he reversed the process, rubbing her clitoris tenderly with his finger while his tongue sought to enter her. Rebecca moaned and bucked her hips as he brought her nearer and nearer to her climax. Watching, Julia felt her own arousal becoming unbearable too. She reached beneath her skirt and found the damp cloth of her panties, under which her sex was swollen and streaming. Putting one finger in through the leg she touched her overheated pussy with a long 'Aaah!' and began to play with herself, pushing beyond her plump outer and inner lips to where the aching, molten flesh gave way to her vaginal opening.

Before Julia could get very far, however, Rebecca had her on-screen orgasm. She was squeezing her thighs together over Marlon's penetrating hand while he sucked at her nipples, prolonging her climax. Julia watched him pull out his gleaming fingers and stroke her stomach, then give her a light

11

kiss on the forehead before covering her body with a lightweight towel.

'I'll leave you to rest now, Miss Maitland,' he murmured. 'When you're ready the showers are just through there and the changing room beyond.'

'Yes, thank you,' she whispered, faintly. Then, as if afraid of seeming ungrateful she added, more loudly, 'Thank you, Marlon, very much indeed!'

Julia switched off the screen. Another satisfied customer! Moving through the door opposite into her own private sauna and plunge pool, she stripped off her clothes and was soon lying naked on the wooden slats, luxuriating in the heat. She gave a deep sigh and let her hands move down to her bare breasts. She clasped them from beneath, proud of their jutting firmness. Not many women could boast of breasts as large and firm as hers without implants. They hardly flopped as she lay down but remained proud and taut, the dark pink nipples beginning to change from relaxed softness to puckered arousal. Julia scratched them gently with her long nails, feeling the mysterious pulse somewhere between her nipples and her womb begin its insistent throbbing. The sauna always made her feel randy and, following what she had just seen, her blood was fired with more than usual heat. Julia remembered the selection of sex toys that she kept in a box in the corner. A little gentle stimulation would do for now, just to keep her ticking over.

Julia reached for the catch and the lid of the box flew open, revealing the various dildoes, vibrators and other aids to sexual pleasure that she had collected for her personal use. She had long ceased feeling guilty about having them. After her marriage to Leo had ended, sex had become of little more significance to her than an itch needing an

12

occasional scratch, and these toys allowed her to save her physical and emotional energy for what mattered most: her work.

She selected a long, slim dildo in natural-feel latex, nothing too fancy or hi-tech, and settled down into a corner with her legs spread wide. One hand lazily squeezed her breast while the other applied the tip of the fake phallus to her clitoris. She shuddered as the first teasing thrills raced round her loins, reassuring her that satisfaction was not far off. Mentally she was reliving the scene with Marlon and Rebecca, feeling her own arousal intensify as she remembered the girl's swift rise towards orgasm. Now she could feel Marlon's capable hands cajoling her own flesh into warm submission, the plastic tool becoming his finger on her button, expert, relentless in its pursuit of her climax.

Julia sighed and shifted position, letting the artificial glans nose inside her opening and pushing the shaft hard against her uptilted mons. The electric vibrations were mimicked by the throbbing of her own sex as she thrust slowly in and out, her hips moving in sync with her hand, her other fingers pulling more urgently on her firmed nipples. She began to moan softly as the sensations moved her up a notch, the heat-induced relaxation of her body changing subtly into the tenser posture of a woman fast approaching orgasm.

'Oh God!' she groaned, when the relentless probing of the dildo achieved its goal, making her clasp it rhythmically with her inner walls in the wild ecstacy of release. She pressed her thighs tightly together to prolong the delicious sensations until, flinging the toy aside like a bored child, she settled down exhausted to wallow in the afterglow.

Surely this was the perfect solution to those occasional twinges, Julia told herself: steamy videos on tap, a private sauna and a collection of sophisticated gadgets guaranteed to bring her to orgasm with maximum efficiency. So why did she always feel so desolate after one of these sessions? Her body was satisfied but another, less accessible, part of her remained empty. What did she want – a man? God forbid, after Leo! Been there, done that. Or rather, been done to. Julia gave a brief shudder at the thought of her ex-husband's domineering ways. She couldn't run the risk of any man having that kind of hold over her again. It wasn't so much what he'd done to her physically as the way he'd undermined all her confidence.

Well, she'd certainly managed to build up her self-esteem again since her divorce. Thinking of the success of *Sybarites* she gave a smile. Tomorrow she'd be interviewing for Warren's replacement. She had been sorry to lose one of her best staff, but the lure of an all-male health club on the other side of town had been too strong for him. Finding someone to match him was proving tricky, since the three candidates she'd already seen had been so unsuitable they hadn't even got past first base. The latest applicant looked far more promising but, in the end, there was only one way to tell whether a masseur was good at his job and that was to try him out herself. To feel a man's hands working with professional sensuality on her body, without any messy emotional involvement, would be a treat. And when, as invariably occurred, he failed to perform to her complete satisfaction, Julia could always pop into the sauna again – she couldn't wait!

Chapter Two

IT WAS EARLY afternoon when Julia had the call from reception to tell her that Grant Delaney had arrived. 'Send him over, Steven,' she replied.

Settling back in her chair she removed the man's photo from his file and studied it for a few seconds. If the camera could be believed he was good-looking, always an asset in their business. At thirty-two he appeared still to have a full head of hair. He had a sexy mouth and intelligent eyes too – she liked that. Well, seeing would be believing.

The man himself proved to be even more attractive than his photograph. From the moment he walked into Julia's office the atmosphere seemed more vibrant, more alive.

'Hi, I'm Grant Delaney,' he smiled, giving her a warm, firm handshake. Julia was disconcerted by the brilliant blue of his eyes, the colour of a summer sky. By contrast, his hair was entirely black, thick and glossy, without a hint of grey. She wondered if he dyed it.

He sat astride the chair with an air of casual ease, despite the fact that he was wearing a suit. No tie, though. His white shirt was in stark contrast to the navy twill, and he had left the collar open to show

15

his tanned neck. Beneath the jacket Julia could tell his arms and chest were well moulded. Yet he was no arrogant muscle-man. There was a quiet assurance about him, the kind of strength that didn't need to flex its biceps to get respect.

Julia answered his dazzling smile with one of her own. 'I'm Julia Marquis, owner-manager of *Sybarites*. Well, Grant, I've read through your application and you seem to be just the sort of person I'm looking for. Your professional references are good, but do you have any personal references?'

He handed her a letter, folded in two. Julia read through the brief recommendation, with its stock phrases, but when she saw the signature her eyes widened. 'Doreen Cadstock?'

'Yes. As she explains in the note, we met while I was working on board a cruise ship.'

'I see.' It seemed an odd coincidence that the MP's wife had only just joined the club. Odder still that she hadn't mentioned anything about Grant the day before, but maybe she didn't want to seem to be pushing him.

'Well, I suppose we'd better find out if what we do here is the kind of work you'd feel happy doing.'

Julia handed him a brochure and his eyes met hers, side-tracking her momentarily. Time definitely stood still when she looked into those blue depths. She continued to talk, rather too quickly, as he flicked through the illustrated pages.

'What this club is all about, Grant, is pleasure and relaxation. We offer a very special service to those women who want it: complete physical fulfilment. Many of them say they get more sensual gratification here than they do from their own husbands or lovers. You'll see our Intimate Massage service detailed on page twenty-three.'

His face remained impassive as he scanned the

page, with its explicit text and frank photos. Then he looked up and the ghost of a smile hovered around his full, sensual lips.

'Yes, I can quite see why women like coming here – no pun intended!'

Julia smothered a grin: she was trying to be businesslike. 'The question is, whether you feel you can perform this service yourself.'

Grant tossed the brochure back on to her desk. 'Did you want an oral recommendation – from one of my past girlfriends, perhaps?'

This time, Julia couldn't help smiling a little. She felt irrationally relieved he wasn't gay. It wouldn't have seemed right to her that so much sex appeal should be for other men.

'I presume you've only been doing straight massage before.'

'That's correct. But I can assure you I've had plenty of informal experience. I think your clients will find my technique perfectly satisfactory.'

Julia cleared her throat. It was becoming very difficult for her to keep up this front. Something about this man made her want to laugh and flirt with him, to feel less uptight and more . . . sexy. Yes, Grant Delaney made her feel sexy, dammit! Well that was a good sign. If he had this effect on her presumably other women would find him equally arousing.

'I'm sure you'll understand that I can't take that on trust,' she began, hesitantly. 'What I do . . . what I've always done when engaging a new masseur is to try him out myself. As if I were a client, just to test his . . . er . . . skill.'

Why did she feel absurdly as if she were propositioning him? She'd managed to road-test all previous masseurs quite detachedly, mentally awarding them marks out of ten for their prowess.

So why did she have this uneasy feeling that it would be different with Grant?

The look that Grant gave her seemed to strip naked her very soul. He slowly raised one thick, dark eyebrow then said, 'And do you enjoy your work? Does it give you job satisfaction, Miss Marquis – or is it *Mrs* Marquis?'

Was he fishing to see if she was married? Well, it was none of his business! No one at work knew about her private life, or lack of it, and she intended to keep it that way.

Her reply was cool. 'Julia will do. I prefer to be on first name terms with my staff, assuming that you are to join us here. Well, we'd better get on with it. I'll just make sure that Warren's old room is free. Sometimes one of the other staff uses it if we have a rush on.'

Slipping into the viewing room, Julia closed the door behind her then paused, leaning back against it. She was trembling, dammit! What the hell was the matter with her? It wasn't as if this was the first time she'd given a masseur a trial. Actually she remembered her first time very well. It had been with Sylvester, who was still with her. He'd been almost as inhibited about it as she was, but somehow they'd managed to get through it. Poor Sylvester! Still, he'd taken it in good part, and after that she'd found it much easier with the others. Of course none of them had ever satisfied her completely, but that was due to her own sexual quirkiness, not to their lack of technique. To please their egos she'd faked a climax every time, just as she used to with Leo. But, unless the women who frequented *Sybarites* were very good actresses, they all found their intimate massage totally satisfying.

Moving to the screen, Julia tuned in to room sixteen. Good, it was empty. Everything was in

18

readiness, however. A pristine white towel lay, neatly folded, on the couch and a large box of tissues was to hand. The flowers had been changed and there were more clean towels on the rail by the hand basin. Perfect! She set the video to record on that channel before going back into her office.

Grant was standing with his back to her, near the window. She noticed how broad his shoulders were, how long and lean his legs. The thick, glossy hair just brushed his collar as he stood motionless, staring at her erotic Japanese print on the wall.

'Right, then,' she smiled with false brightness when he turned round. 'Shall we go? Warren's room, the one that will be yours if you join us, is in the massage suite on the second floor. All the treatment rooms are up there. The pool, gym and healthfood bar are the only facilities on the ground floor.'

She chose to lead him up the stairs rather than take the lift. Although she rationalised it as being the healthier option, part of her knew she was avoiding having to stand too close to him in a confined space. Ridiculous, seeing as how she was about to bare all and let him caress her entire body.

From the phone on the wall outside room twenty-three, Julia buzzed reception.

'Steven, I shall be with Mr Delaney in Warren's room for the next hour. See that I'm not disturbed, will you? Short of a fire, of course. Did Thomson see you about those smoke alarms, by the way?'

Julia found she was glad of the small interlude of neutral business. Once she put the phone down, however, there was nothing to be done but enter the room in front of them. Grant waited patiently as she pointed out the various things he would need.

'Massage oils, creams and talcs are kept in this cupboard,' she explained, trying to sound casual.

'Some women prefer aromatherapy oils, so we keep diluted bottles of those too. We don't expect you to be an expert, of course. Mostly your clients will know themselves what they want, or you can contact Jason, our aromatherapist, who works here three days a week.'

'Fine. I have used them before.'

'This massage couch is specially designed,' she continued. 'Under here you'll find a lever that will open out the end into two halves, so you can get closer to the client's body.'

She demonstrated and, with a faint whirring, the lower end split apart to an angle of forty-five degrees.

'Very impressive!' he grinned. 'And useful, of course.'

'One more thing . . . ' Julia felt herself begin to shake again, and tensed her body. 'All the masseurs work semi-naked. You'll find a clean G-string in that drawer. I hope you've no objections to that?'

He moved to the drawer and removed the scrap of black satin. Holding it up and eyeing it with amusement he said, 'Do you want a strip-tease, too?'

Julia wanted to laugh. Instead she pursed her mouth and swept aside the curtain that concealed an alcove with a chair, mirror and clothes hangers.

'This changing cubicle is for the women. I'll use it today and you can change out here. Take a couple of hangers.'

'Fine.'

Julia was aware that she had been avoiding his eye for the last few minutes, but now she clocked him briefly and gave a weak smile before disappearing behind the curtain. Inside the cubicle she collapsed on to the chair, alarmed at how fast her heart was beating. Take a grip, she told herself as she took off her shoes.

When she emerged, wearing the white towelling

robe, Grant had not quite finished changing. Julia had a brief glimpse of his tawny penis before he tucked it into the black pouch. It was long and thick, and just aroused enough to show the pink glans peeping out from beneath the foreskin. She felt a brief tremor inside, as if an invisible hand had clutched at her womb. Grant looked up and smiled, but then his manner became entirely professional.

'Ah, Ms Marquis. If you'd like to just take off your robe and lie face down on the couch, I'll be with you in a moment.'

Julia did as she was told, aware that Grant was surveying his options in the cupboard. The couch was firm but well padded beneath her body, and she sank into it with a sigh of contentment. Sometimes she didn't realise how exhausted she was until she came to rest.

'Do you prefer an oil, cream or powder, Ms Marquis?' she heard him say.

'Aromatherapy oil, please.'

'Hm . . . Yes, I think this one's for you. Ylang ylang and lavender, very soothing.'

Also very sensual, Julia thought. She was pleased. He'd picked out her favourite combination.

'You seem a little uptight,' he commented from beside the couch as he poured the oil into his cupped palm. 'I'm going to give you a deep muscle massage on your back and buttocks. Hopefully, by the time you turn over you'll be less tense.'

Even the tone of his voice was relaxing, Julia decided. It sounded warm, deep and intelligent. If that was a true reflection of his personality Grant Delaney was quite a guy!

From the first touch, Julia knew she was in safe hands. He smoothed the oil lightly over her shoulders, back and buttocks and she felt her flesh tingle deliciously at the erotic touch of his fingers.

He was standing to one side of her still and, if she opened her eyes just a crack and looked at him through the dark curtain of her lashes, she could see the long, upward-slanting bulge in his pouch.

If he gets an erection while he's working, that silly little pocket won't accommodate him, Julia thought, making a mental note to have a larger size provided. Then she realised that she was thinking of Grant as if he were already a member of her staff.

Soon he was kneading her buttocks with his knuckles, pressing firmly into the springy flesh that she had honed to lean perfection in the gym. A warmth was spreading all through her pelvic region and with it a heavy languor that allowed all tension to seep from her pores, leaving her free to enjoy the intriguing scent of the oil, that was both soothing and stimulating. Like sex itself, she thought.

'You're in good shape,' she heard Grant say, somewhere in the distance.

'Mm.'

He began to slap her bottom all over, with lightly stinging taps of his fingers, toning the muscles. Julia was startled at first but soon relaxed and began to enjoy it. Then, when her behind felt hot and tingling with the keen stimulation, he slowed the pace again and began to make gentle tracks up her back with his fingertips. Down he came again with the flat of his palms, pausing briefly to caress her still-smarting cheeks and then moving up her spine with delicate feathering strokes.

At first Julia found his changes of approach somewhat disconcerting but after a while she began to revel in it, knowing she could trust him. Instead of trying to anticipate what he would do next she gave herself up to the sensations, letting her body take over from her mind until she was almost entirely centred in her flesh.

Now Grant was embracing the backs of her legs with his large hands, his thumbs grazing her inner thighs as he smoothed his way up from her knees to her behind, finishing with a squeeze of her slack buttocks. Julia felt the hypersensitive skin tingle and the first stirrings of real desire flooded through her as those firm thumbs approached her moist crevice and then – oh, so tantalisingly! – retreated again. She wriggled a little against the couch, feeling the firm cushion against her breasts and stomach, grinding her impatient mons against the padding.

'Relax!' Grant murmured, his voice as soothing as his hands. 'There's plenty of time.'

Julia complied at once, not wanting him to break the silence again. She sank like a rag doll into the couch, feeling the warm hands stroke her calves into submission and then start on her feet. Grant poured more oil into his palms and raised her foot so that he could get at both sides at once. Julia loved having her foot tenderly cradled between his careful hands, the slight ticklishness she felt at first soon fading into comfortable sensuality.

When Grant had probed gently all over the soles of her feet with his thumbs he placed one leg across the other as a signal for her to turn over. As she did so, Julia caught sight of the bulge in his pouch and felt a distinct quiver somewhere in the region of her womb. She was faintly disturbed that she had reacted with such involuntary excitement at the sight of it. After all, for the purpose of a client's satisfaction, a masseur's penis should be regarded as totally redundant. Had she made a mistake in decreeing that they should work almost naked? Perhaps that would be just too much of a temptation for some women.

Despite herself Julia peeped at the forbidden organ once again, led by a kind of primitive fascination. Its thickness was over-filling the inadequate scrap of material and, as she had guessed, the pink tip was just peeping over the elasticated band at the top. She closed her eyes to blot out the image.

Grant was manipulating her toes now, rubbing them between his finger and thumb and slotting his little finger into the gaps between them where the skin was hardly ever touched. The effect was very stimulating. Julia breathed deeply, taking in the aromatic air around her, feeling her whole being submerge itself again in the silent, but intense, world of the senses. She felt the capable hands rise up her shins, play with her knees for a bit then massage 'her thighs with firm upward strokes, always stopping short of her groin. The ache in her womb intensified, grew more insistent the more he repeated the slow stimulation of her thighs while studiously avoiding all contact with her pubic area. Soon he had by-passed it altogether, coming to stand behind her head so that he could massage her face.

For a few seconds Julia's sexual arousal dropped, to be replaced by slight disappointment. But Grant's delicate caressing of her cheeks and brow was exquisitely soothing. He was making small circling motions, gently moving the soft flesh over the bones beneath until all the tiny electric tensions were discharged. Then he was pinching along the firm line of her jaw with both hands, and tracing the contours of her ears, lightly invading the orifices with his fingertips. He moved down to caress her neck with sweeping upward strokes, but as his attention turned to her shoulders Julia felt the first tingles of her reawakened desire, aware that, just below, her sensitive breasts lay open to his touch.

He took his time getting there. After some light

kneading of her shoulders Grant moved to her arms and hands, making a thorough job of massaging every digit. Then he addressed the flat plane of her stomach, traversing it with his palms in long, rhythmic strokes. He slowly widened his range until the outer edge of one hand was just brushing the top of her pubic hair, while the other came into fleeting contact with the lower edge of her breasts.

Julia found this light flirtation with her erogenous zones incredibly tantalising. Her desire was thoroughly re-kindled now, and she knew that if he played 'blow hot, blow cold' with her for much longer she wouldn't be able to stand it. At the beginning she had trusted him to know what he was doing, but if he failed her now . . .

There was a familiar whirring noise as the couch divided below her hips and Julia felt her legs being thrust open. She was aware that Grant had come to stand between her parted thighs, and his hands were moving up from her midriff to encircle her breasts. He was working all round the outside edge of her globes, feathering her skin, making the nipples swell into aching tumescence before he'd even touched them. She could feel his knuckles against the taut slopes as he made his teasing progress round and round, massaging her ribcage.

Then, almost imperceptibly, he had moved to touching the breasts themselves. Julia was glad they were capable of standing proud and full, wondered what Grant thought of them as he began to give them his undivided attention. She found she wanted him to admire them, to gain pleasure from handling them. He had them in his hands now, ripe and warm, and he was kneading them – no longer like a masseur, but like a lover, signalling at some subliminal level that the nature of the business had subtly changed. It had been such a smooth transition from the sensual to the erotic that Julia couldn't help feeling she was in the hands of an expert, despite his assurance that he'd never done this before. He must be a good lover, she thought, and was amazed at the accompanying feeling of jealousy that came out of nowhere. What was it to her how many women he'd practised on before? She was judging his professional expertise, not his seduction technique, she reminded herself.

Yet that distinction, too, began to blur once he began to work on her nipples, rolling, flicking, tugging, until they tingled with rampant life. Julia knew she was wet down below, knew that her clitoris was as hard and tingling as the nipples he was so expertly teasing, and she longed for him to unfold her sex, to gently probe between the labia and find the swollen bud where her hunger was keenest. Her breath was coming out ragged between faint moans as he alternated his pace: now softly caressing the lower slopes of her breasts, where the skin was ultra-sensitive, now grasping great handfuls of her flesh and squeezing, while roughly thumbing her nipples. Sometimes he would make a great sweep downward past her naval to brush his palm across her bush, and then her hips would jerk involuntarily as a spasm shook her, deep inside.

Then the downward strokes became more frequent, and his forefinger pressed at the very top of her sex where the nub of her greatest pleasure lay – only for a second at a time, but it was enough to cause her juices to flow more copiously. Grant let his finger slide into her momentarily, as if to test the dampness, before returning to caress her breasts. Julia wondered how much longer she would have to endure this indirect stimulation. Already her breasts felt at bursting point and her clitoris was pulsating away like a small generator.

Grant's hands moved to her upper thighs and she felt his thumbs just touch the plump outer lips as he made small circles with his knuckles in her groin. Through half-closed lids she could look right down her body and see him standing there, between her spread thighs, his eyes lowered, intent on the job. The muscled contours of his arms and chest were lightly tanned, his hands working rhythmically to bring her pleasure, pressing more firmly now against the warm cushion of her labia.

Glancing down, Julia saw the sideways bulge of his prick still filling the black pouch and she shuddered inwardly. Somehow it seemed all wrong that she should be lying there taking all but giving nothing. The urge to uncover his sex, to take it between her hands and caress it to its full length and girth, came upon her suddenly and she dismissed it quickly as a foolish fantasy, reminding herself of who she was and what this encounter was about. Briefly, she assessed his progress. So far Grant Delaney was scoring well, very well indeed.

Just as Julia closed her eyes again she was aware of a change in Grant's posture. She peeped to see him squatting, his head on a level with her groin, and a new wave of anticipation passed through her with a deliciously expectant thrill. His fingers gently parted her labia and then she could feel the cool pressure of his tongue in her groove, licking its way slowly inwards until it was probing at the very entrance to her vagina. After a few seconds it continued upwards until, finding the fleshy nub it was seeking, the tip of Grant's tongue flicked back and forth with practised ease over the sensitive spot. Unable to help herself, Julia groaned aloud.

The rest all happened very fast. Grant's tongue and fingers came into play in smooth accord, and Julia felt her wet pussy being explored all along its velvet length while her clitoris grew hot and slick with his saliva. Soon she was wriggling sensually, out of control, as the unstoppable build-up towards a climax began. Normally she would be holding back at this time, unwilling – or unable – to let herself tip over the edge into abandonment. This time, though, she knew she would go the whole way. Revelling in the mindless journey of her flesh, Julia felt him change over, his mouth at the streaming entrance while one stiff finger ground the slippery peak of her lust.

It was enough to trigger her. Julia felt the first tremors come as a warm fluttering from deep within, building rapidly to great pumping waves of hot ecstasy. She was faintly aware of him stroking her thighs and stomach, spreading the sensations down towards her knees and up to her breasts. The orgasm went on and on, so that she began to wonder whether it would ever stop or would she have to live out the rest of her life in perpetual bliss, like some latter-day saint. Then the wild pulsations began to diminish and she scorned her foolish imaginings. She had come, that was all. But that was not all. The wondrous fact was that she had allowed a man to make her come, for the first time in her life.

Even so, she felt oddly cheated. Why couldn't such a momentous event have happened at another time, in another place, and with a man she knew well instead of this total stranger? It didn't make sense. Women were supposed to respond most deeply to an act of love, not to some kind of clinical trial.

It was ridiculous how nervous Julia felt afterwards, how like a coy schoolgirl and how unlike a fully-grown independent businesswoman. She lay inert while Grant gently wiped her with a moist tissue and removed the oils from his hands with a paper towel. Her mind still inhabited the realm of the senses that her body was slowly leaving, and she found it impossible to rise briskly and get back to business. Grant seemed to sense this.

'Excuse me while I wash my hands,' he murmured, his voice low and mellow, scarcely disturbing her silence. Julia lay on, limp but glowing, while she considered his performance. She would have to give him ten out of ten, of course. And that meant she would have to take him on. So why did she felt a pang of disquiet at the thought?

Rising from the couch while his back was turned, Julia said she was going to take a shower and disappeared through the side door. The enlivening play of water on her body soon had her mind focused again so that by the time she emerged, swathed in a white towel, she was able to say to Grant quite casually, 'Your turn now. I'll see you back in my office in ten minutes or so.'

She caught his eye, briefly, and the look of frank enquiry in its blue depths startled her so that she scurried into the cubicle and drew the curtain across. After dressing quickly she ran a brush through her tangled, dark blonde hair until it clung to her head in sculpted waves. She sprayed herself with a light perfume as if, by doing so, she could hide the lingering scent of her recent passion, then left the room, her exit masked by the noise of running water.

Alone in her office, Julia set about trying to resurrect the image of efficient manager. She sat behind the barrier of her desk, wondering what she would say to Grant when he appeared. Of course, he would do as Warren's replacement. There was no question of that. Yet something in her had changed, irrevocably, and he was the man responsible. Unbeknown to him he had acquired a secret power over her, but she must never ever let on or he might take advantage. Julia had fought hard for sole control of *Sybarites*, her authority was unquestioned by her staff and her clients admired her obvious success in a tricky field. She could never allow anyone to upset that status quo.

So when Grant knocked at her door, Julia called 'Come in!' with the peremptory tone of a headmistress about to interview a difficult pupil. The cheeky look he threw her as he entered, however, almost destroyed her carefully prepared front.

'Well, will I do?' he enquired, directly he had sat opposite her. His dark brows were quizzically raised, and as Julia glanced down to avoid his gaze she couldn't help seeing his capable brown hands lying loosely in his lap, the very hands that had brought her to a climax only minutes before. To her horror, she felt a tell-tale flush rise in her cheeks.

'I should think so,' she replied brusquely, hiding her face by searching in her desk drawer. She pulled out a contract and handed it to him. 'Take this away and read it through. There were one or two minor points I wanted to make about your ... er ... technique, but they can wait till next time.'

'I would rather know right away, if you don't mind.' His voice was light, but insistent. 'I think the closer a debriefing is held to the event the better, don't you?'

He's trying to tell me my job, she thought, angrily.

'Very well.' Her tone was tinged with sudden frost. 'Firstly, I think it's best to avoid speech altogether once the massage has begun, unless it's absolutely necessary of course.'

'I agree,' he smiled. 'It ruins the relaxed atmosphere. I don't know why I said anything. I was probably nervous.'

'Then you hid it well. I thought your technique was

good too, although at times you seemed a bit too . . . rough.'

'Sometimes you need to increase the blood flow quickly to a certain part of the body,' he explained. 'When I worked on your buttocks, for example, or stimulated your breasts.'

Julia couldn't believe he was talking so coolly about such intimate matters. Was that all she'd been to him, a backside and a pair of boobs? She knew it was unreasonable to expect any more of him, and yet surely he had been moved in some way by the strength of her passion?

'Well, your techniques certainly worked, as you no doubt realised.'

She threw him an uncharacteristically coy look, instantly despising herself for doing so. He smiled the smile of a man who knows he has satisfied his woman, and Julia rose abruptly, barking her shin on the leg of the desk as she did so. Cursing inwardly, she fixed her lips in a grin that was more than half grimace, and held out her hand.

'Once you've read through the contract we can have another chat about conditions and so forth. Shall we say . . . tomorrow at ten?'

'That'll be fine.'

He held her hand a fraction longer than she expected, just long enough to make it feel slightly imprisoned in his larger grasp. Then he moved directly towards the door and was gone.

Chapter Three

JULIA HAD HAD a restless night. Somehow the effect of Grant's massage had been to revive old insecurities about her relationships with men. In the space of one hour she had allowed him to get nearer to the secret, sensual heart of her than her husband had done in five years, and her hard won self-sufficiency had been rocked to the core.

Memories of her unhappy marriage to Leo returned to torment her as she drove to the club next morning. Julia had been a virgin of nineteen when she'd married him, all starry-eyed and acquiescent. Forty years old, rich and successful, Leo had been the father-figure she'd never had. Her mother, Sally, had made love with a fellow hippie during an LSD trip and fallen pregnant, so that Julia was truly a child of the Sixties. When the dream was over there had been no question of marriage but Sally had embraced the role of single mother enthusiastically, drawing strength from the burgeoning Women's Movement in the Seventies. She had disapproved strongly of Julia's relationship with Leo.

'That man has you completely under his thumb,' she'd complained. 'You'll never have any life or personality of your own if you marry him.'

At the time Julia had put her mother's sourness down to envy. Her theory was that having struggled to bring up a child on her own, Sally couldn't bear the idea that her daughter would have a conventionally happy marriage. Yet within a few months, Julia began to suspect that her mother had been right. Leo made it clear from the start that he would be making all the main decisions. He had bought them a house, given her a car, taken her on a 'surprise' honeymoon trip to Jamaica. On their wedding night they had made love by moonlight surrounded by the scent of gardenias, but although Leo had taken time to arouse her the act of intercourse had left her cold. She had pretended to be rapturously happy and fully satisfied, telling herself that it was early days yet and their lovemaking would get better. But having faked orgasm on the first occasion Julia felt obliged to do it again and again, until the lie had become too established to shift.

When Leo had opened 'Hammond's Health Club' he had reluctantly agreed to allow Julia to work there as a part-time receptionist. Slowly she'd taken over more of the running of the place until she had turned it into a thriving business, trebling the membership in six months. Perhaps it had been her new-found confidence in her own abilities that had given Julia the strength to divorce Leo. She'd never admitted that she found their sex-life unsatisfying, but instead had blamed the breakdown of their marriage on the many business interests that kept him away from home. She hadn't dared accuse him of what she suspected, that he'd slept with other women on his frequent 'business trips'.

'But I only wanted to give you a better standard of living,' he'd moaned.

Julia had said, 'It was you I wanted, not houses and cars,' but even as she'd spoken the words she knew she had uttered another lie, to soothe his battered ego. She'd never really wanted Leo. He had presented himself to her on a plate when she was young and suggestible enough to fall for his worldly charm, but she'd never *wanted* him.

Not the way she wanted Grant. The unwelcome truth hit her at the very instant that the traffic lights turned red. Julia drew up sharply, finding the warning light symbolic. She reminded herself that she was bound to feel a strong attraction for someone who had pleasured her as much as he had, but it didn't mean she should do anything about it. She'd always known that in setting up *Sybarites* as a club where women could be serviced by male masseurs she was morally sailing close to the wind. Despite the fact that she'd earned herself a grudging respect from the business community, even becoming a member of the Chamber of Commerce, Julia was still subjected to occasional innuendo by the 'nudge, nudge, wink, wink' brigade. So she had to be careful that no breath of real scandal sullied the reputation of the club, and she herself must be above reproach. Although not even royalty can claim to be that these days, she thought wryly, gliding forward as the lights changed to green.

By ten o'clock she had armed herself against Grant's reappearance with an air of cool efficiency – or so she thought. His entrance into her office knocked her sideways. Instead of the smart suit of yesterday he was wearing jeans with a T-shirt and looking far too approachable. He brought with him a faint aura of Dior's *Fahrenheit*, which did nothing to reduce her temperature. Julia felt a brief shudder in her belly, kick-starting her sexual reflexes. Beneath the tailored formality of her jacket and crisply laundered blouse her breasts were straining for release, and her smooth, Lycra-clad thighs shifted restlessly.

'Hope you don't mind the informal clothes,' he grinned as he sat down. 'I was planning on using the gym later, if that's okay.'

'Yes, of course. The masseurs are entitled to free use of all the facilities after hours, as indicated in your contract.'

In her effort to remain detached, Julia sounded ridiculously pompous. Grant's grin widened. 'It's a pity you don't employ any female masseuses. We males like being pampered too, you know. Incidentally, why *did* you turn this club into women only? I gather it used to be mixed.'

Julia had been asked this question many times, and her reply came out pat.

'I think men have had it all their own way for too long. I wanted to create an atmosphere where women could enjoy guilt-free sensuality without risk. The inhabitants of the ancient Greek community of Sybaris were famous for their luxurious lifestyle. That's why I've named my masseurs after Hollywood idols, since that's the modern equivalent of that legendary city.'

'So you want me to change my name. What to – Cary, perhaps?'

Julia laughed. 'Actually I think "Grant" is rather good. A combination of Hollywood heart-throb and Civil War general. I'm not sure we could better it.'

'That's fine by me. I was afraid you might want to call me "Woody" or "Pee Wee" and that wouldn't have done much for my reputation.'

Despite her amusement, Julia was suddenly alert. 'Reputation?' She fingered the file containing his references, including Doreen Cadstock's letter. 'I do hope you've never been accused of professional misconduct. I have to be so careful, you see. I must stress that in signing that contract you agree to abide strictly by the rules of the club.'

His eyes slid momentarily away from hers before returning her gaze again with frank brilliance. 'I understand completely, Julia. And you can rest assured that my credentials are good. I just meant that my standing amongst my colleagues might not be so good if you gave me some dubious name.'

'I wouldn't dream of doing anything to make your settling in here difficult,' she answered rather sharply. 'You'll start on three months' probation, with a week's notice on either side.'

The talk passed to ordinary matters but Julia was aware of an undercurrent to their conversation. She suspected that he might be remembering how her skin felt under his caress, just as she was. No matter how hard she tried to forget their more intimate relations, turning her mind to weekend rotas and time off in lieu, her body was responding to his at a basic, animal level. She could feel his magnetic presence pulling at the tides of her being, drawing out the secret fluids from her hidden springs. The damp heat in the gusset of her tights made her squirm uncomfortably in her seat while she strove to keep her voice at an even pitch.

'Was there anything else?' Julia asked at last, and let out a relieved breath when he shook his head. 'Then do go and use the gym, by all means. I shall tell Steven at Reception that you are available for booking from tomorrow. Maybe later today you'd like to be introduced to some of your colleagues?'

'Yes, that would be nice.'

He smiled, rising and offering his hand. The brief contact threatened Julia's composure as she recalled exactly where those long, smooth fingers had been.

Am I making a terrible mistake, she asked herself as she watched his broad back disappear through her door.

Her phone buzzed: it was Steven, saying the solar heating man was waiting in Reception to see her. Julia was grateful for the distraction. For the next half hour she discussed the possibility of partially heating the club's water with solar panels, taking the man up to survey the flat roof of the building and allowing him to inspect the plumbing. It was a job she could have left entirely to her staff but she hadn't made *Sybarites* what it was today by sitting on the sidelines. It was a matter of pride that she should involve herself personally with every aspect of the club's management.

They had to pass the gym on the way to the boiler room. Julia glanced through the window and saw Grant at his exercise station, pounding away on the 'Pec Deck'. A turquoise singlet and pair of navy shorts showed off his body to perfection, the lightly-tanned skin moulded tautly over the working muscles.

Julia's eyes dropped briefly to his strong thighs and she remembered that she had to order him a larger G-string. The memory of his briefly-glimpsed organ returned, uncensored, sending ripples of alarming intensity through her lower body. She turned away to see the eyes of the solar heating engineer regarding her with curiosity.

'You look as if you work out in the gym too, Miss Marquis,' the man said, his eyes blatantly examining her figure. 'I suppose that when you run a health club you have to be a good advertisement yourself.'

'I try my best to be,' she smiled, distantly, before changing the subject with a technical question.

When the engineer had gone and Julia had a few moments free in her office, she went into the viewing room and switched on the gym's monitor. Grant was on the running machine now, his body in a relaxed rhythm, but in the background she could see Rebecca and Lou, the two models, eyeing him up in the mirror and giggling to each other as they worked out side by side on the rowing machines. Julia frowned. Normally the masseurs only used the gym after work, when they could have it to themselves. Had she made a mistake in letting Grant use it in full view of two of her youngest and most impressionable clients?

Her answer came next day, when she asked Steven if anyone had booked Grant for a massage yet.

'Yes, a booking was made yesterday,' he smiled, scrolling through the appointments for her to see on screen. 'Two o'clock. Miss Lou Marsh.'

'I knew it!' Julia thought, sourly. While she talked shop with Steven her mind was still working on the information she'd just received. That girl had the hots for Grant, it was obvious. No doubt she'd been discussing her chances with Rebecca yesterday, as they ogled him in the gym. Not that she could blame her, but could she trust Grant to keep their relationship on a strictly professional basis? As his first client, the young, attractive model would be a real test of his ability to separate business and pleasure – especially if she fancied him something rotten.

'Steve, I shall be incommunicado between two and three today,' she informed him. 'I have to look over some spreadsheets before the VAT inspector calls next week, and I don't want to be disturbed, okay?'

'Yes, Miss Julia,' he grinned. For one nasty moment she wondered if he suspected anything, but then told herself she was being silly. Besides, she really did have to go through the records sometime soon.

As two o'clock approached, Julia was feeling ridiculously on edge. She had watched many novice masseurs with their first clients before, but somehow this was different. It was hard to convince herself that her interest was purely that of an employer checking on a new employee. Her palms were clammy, her pulse-rate up and there was a leaden feeling around her heart like indigestion. Added to which, the mere thought of what she was about to witness was firming up her breasts while softening her up inside, making the sensitive tissues swell and moisten.

Suddenly the door of the massage room opened and Grant entered, moving purposefully across the room and unbuttoning his shirt as he went.

'Oh, Grant!'

His name had slipped out with a sigh, before Julia could stop it. Watching him perform his unconscious strip-tease she felt her spine tingle with delicious anticipation, just as if it were she, and not Lou, who was about to get up on that couch and place her body in his expert hands.

Grant had his back to her as he slipped on the new G-string so that all Julia saw were his lean-sculpted buttocks. He's been on the sunbed, she thought, noticing there was no 'visible panty line'. Either that or he had a secluded garden to sunbathe in. Julia began idly speculating about his private life. She knew from his application form that he was single, but that meant nothing these days. Did he have a live-in girlfriend? If he wasn't long off the cruise ships it was more likely he'd played the field. Was 'a girl in every port' more his style? Suddenly a bleak emptiness gripped her heart, along with a pang of self-disgust. What was she doing, fantasising about the man as if he were a potential lover?

Just then there came a tentative knock at the door of the massage room. Grant strode to open it and Lou entered, closely followed by Rebecca. Lou said something, flashing him a practised smile, and Grant looked rather surprised. Since Julia hadn't gone to the extent of having the room bugged – there had seemed no need for it – she could only guess at their conversation. Without batting an eyelid Lou said something apparently even more outageous, and Julia could see that Grant looked shocked. The girls giggled. Lou put her bag down in the corner and Rebecca followed suit. They were both very attractive, Lou the shorter and more shapely of the two with seductive green eyes and blonde hair, while Rebecca was dark and on the skinny side. Together they made a formidable team and one which, Julia guessed, few men could resist.

Julia saw that he was tempted by Lou's proposition, whatever it was. She could almost hear him thinking 'Why not?' Even so it was tough to be put on the spot on his first job. She almost felt sorry for him.

At last he shrugged his assent. They giggled like schoolgirls and each kissed Grant on the cheek before starting to strip in front of him. He indicated the changing cubicle, but they shrugged and continued to undress in his sight. Obviously their work had made them accustomed to strippping in front of men. Lou got up on to the massage couch and then Rebecca gave a wicked grin, springing up beside her friend. The pair lay there like figures on an ancient tomb while Grant gave them the choice of massage oil.

'So that's their game!' Julia muttered. They wanted him to do them both at the same time.

Cheeky minxes! At the touch of the button the lower half of the couch divided, so that Rebecca's legs went one way and Lou's the other, allowing Grant to get between them.

The giggling subsided once they were face down on the couch, their round, pink bottoms presented to the air. Rebecca let out a long sigh as she wiggled into a more relaxed position. To Julia's surprise, the couch accommodated the pair of them easily. They were so thin that the padded top, which had been designed to suit all body shapes and sizes, allowed them to lie side by side with a few inches to spare.

Fascinated as she was by the sight, Julia was still shocked to see them there together. Grant rubbed his oiled palms together before placing a palm on each of their backs, his right hand moving clockwise over Rebecca while his left massaged Lou in the opposite direction. Both girls appeared thoroughly relaxed now, and Grant began to get into his stride, travelling up and down their spines with his knuckles, kneading their taut buttocks and smoothing down their slim thighs until every inch of their backs and legs was covered with a sleek, scented film.

Julia stared intently at the screen, her mind in a whirl. Obviously Grant was breaking the rules, and on his very first job. She knew she should do something, but what? If she interrupted their session now, by phone or personal intervention, that would be tantamount to admitting she was spying on them. Could she barge in by accident, invent some pretext? It was tempting, but Julia doubted whether she could carry it off convincingly. Maybe she'd wait until they came out of the room and accost them in the corridor. Yes, that was her best plan. Meanwhile, she would continue to observe the trio through the closed circuit camera in

41

case Grant was seduced into breaking any more rules of her establishment, written or unwritten.

It was far from easy, though, to remain a helpless voyeur while Grant and his two willing accomplices continued their illicit game. Once the two girls had turned over and Grant began caressing their feet, Julia felt her own toes itch with longing for similar treatment. So vivid was the memory of his touch that her feet were responding as if it were happening to them for real. She kicked off her shoes and scrunched her toes into the carpet just to feel something tangible, and the rough texture of the wool pile through her tights was almost enough.

Almost, but not quite. As Grant's hands travelled up the girls' shins simultaneously, Julia's own hands mimicked his movements. Soon he was circling over their twin bellies, Rebecca's flat as a pancake and Lou's rather more rounded. His motion spread upwards until he was skirting Rebecca's small boobs, crested with their immature pink tips, and at the same time nudging the undersides of Lou's ampler breasts, their red nipples well roused and clamouring for attention. Julia rubbed her own breasts over her thin blouse, feeling them swell and harden.

This is no good, she told herself, suddenly ashamed of her wanton disregard for duty. She walked briskly back into her office, pressed a few buttons to summon up her spreadsheet, and sat down, intending to get on with some work.

If she craned her neck to peer through the open doorway into her private viewing room Julia could still see the tormenting figures, but she did her best to ignore them. The figures on the screen before her should have been far more alluring, telling their tale of success after success. In November Julia had added a new suite of rooms so that they could accommodate more members and, although they weren't yet functioning to capacity, the membership growth rate was highly satisfactory. Her bank manager was very pleased with her.

And what of Leo? He knew how she had developed his initial venture and must have heard of its growth through the grapevine. Was he pleased with his ex-wife's success, or did he take a sour grapes attitude? During their brief encounters at meetings of the Chamber of Commerce neither had given much away.

It was no good – she had to take another look. Julia pushed back her chair and moved to the doorway. Now Grant was bringing both girls to a climax with his fingers while his tongue flicked across first Rebecca's small nipple, then Lou's larger one. They were squirming in delight, hips wriggling, toes wiggling, their wet lips parted probably to let out sighs and moans of utter abandonment to the expert manipulations of the masseur.

Julia regarded the scene with disgust. Had she really let him do similar things to her, only yesterday? He'd given her the most exquisite pleasure she'd ever known from any man, but of course he'd been trying hard to please his prospective boss. She'd been a fool to imagine that he'd gained any personal satisfaction from their session. Today, seeing him behave like the skilled operative he really was, she realised that he had a good technique, that was all, and the sooner she faced facts and quelled her misplaced lust for him the better. Julia sighed. How ironic that she had found the lover of her dreams amongst her own employees. But after her divorce she had vowed to put business before pleasure, and she would continue to do just that.

By the time Rebecca and Lou were getting

43

dressed again, like giggling schoolgirls after a session in the gym, Julia had decided not to confront Grant after all. It had been hard enough to find a replacement for Warren, and he was certainly good at his job. Provided he didn't transgress again she would turn a blind eye on this occasion since no real harm had been done. And if the two models spread the word amongst their friends that *Sybarites* was the best health club in town, so much the better.

Julia had finished her work at the computer and was on her way to see Brad, who ran the Healthfood Bar, when she bumped into Grant at Reception. The sight of his lean body in a relaxed pose, the tight jeans showing off his trim posterior, made her insides flip with involuntary excitement. He was talking to Steve at the desk and she could easily have slipped past without acknowledging him, but she had made up her mind to treat him like any other new employee and that meant making sure he was settling in okay. So she joined the two men with a smile.

'Hullo, Miss Julia,' Steve said at once. 'I was just telling Grant here that he has another booking.'

'Oh, good!' Julia tried hard to sound neutral, even though she could feel her heart beating a wild tattoo under the influence of Grant's wide smile. 'And how did your first session go?'

'Very well indeed, thanks.' If he had any pangs of guilt about his two-for-the-price-of-one act it didn't show in the slightest. 'I think I might even have gained us a few more customers.'

'Members,' Julia corrected him. 'Never forget that this is a health club, Grant, not just a massage parlour. You'll have to get rid of that cruise ship mentality here.'

Her rebuke sounded sharper than she'd intended. For a moment a shadow passed over Grant's brow, and she was afraid he would somehow call her bluff. But then he grinned. 'Thanks for reminding me, *Ms* Julia.'

Despite her intention to remain detached, Julia couldn't resist asking Steve who Grant's next client would be. He knew without looking it up. 'Mrs Cadstock. Tomorrow morning, at ten.'

Julia felt a pang of something absurdly like jealousy. She was about to make some snide reference to the fact that Doreen had given Grant a good recommendation, but she thought better of it. Instead she murmured, 'Good. Well, I must be going. You know where to find me, Grant, if you have any problems.'

But as Julia hurried through the swing doors she couldn't help fearing that, if she continued to respond to his presence like a lovesick schoolgirl, she would be the one with all the problems.

Chapter Four

SINCE JULIA LIKED to keep up with the local news she had the *Gazette* delivered on Fridays. Scanning it over her breakfast she was startled to see the headline 'MP's Anti-Vice Campaign'. A photograph of Jeremy Cadstock and his wife Doreen sent shivers of foreboding down Julia's spine.

It seemed that the MP had made a speech in the Commons calling for something like the 'moral re-armament' movement that had tried to stem the permissive tide of the Sixties. He'd compared Britain's present state to the 'Fall of the Roman Empire' and demanded tougher laws against 'prostitution, pornography, divorce, homosexuality and pederasty'. The fact that both his wife and mistress were members of *Sybarites* was incongruous, to say the least. Did Jeremy Cadstock know that? More to the point, did he know what went on within the club's well protected walls?

Then she remembered that Doreen was due for a massage with Grant that morning. Was it just a coincidence that she had recommended him for the post? Julia frowned, wondering whether she should heed the faint alarm bells that were sounding in her head, but decided she was being paranoid. If

Cadstock was using his wife to spy at *Sybarites* then Julia had a trump card up her sleeve: his mistress. If ever the truth came out about Tanya he would soon be making headline news in the national and not just the local press.

It sickened Julia that she had to think in those terms, but she knew she had to watch her back. Some months ago there had been a nasty incident where a husband had stormed into the club's reception area, thinking his wife was using the place to rendezvous with her lover. Fortunately he had been quickly stopped by Steven and one of the masseurs, and Julia had managed to smooth things over. But she still had nightmares about it. The incident had taught Julia that she couldn't be too careful in vetting prospective members and monitoring how the club was run. If there were any hidden agenda regarding Cadstock's wife and mistress then she would sniff it out and, if necessary, turn it to her advantage.

When Julia arrived that morning, Steven greeted her more soberly than usual.

'Have you seen the front page of the local rag, Miss Julia?'

'About our Right Honorable's latest pronouncements, you mean?' She gave a wry grin.

He raised his finely arched brows at her. 'Faint scent of rodent, don't you think?'

'Maybe. Wifey's due at ten, isn't she? We'll have to see if she keeps her appointment.'

Julia reasoned that if Doreen Cadstock cried off then there might, indeed, be cause for alarm. She didn't, however. Promptly at ten Julia, watching on the CCTV screen, saw Grant open the door of his massage room and usher in the MP's wife They stood for a few seconds, chatting briefly, then Doreen disappeared into the changing cubicle. By

47

the time she emerged, draped in a white towel, Grant had also stripped – but not to his G-string. Instead, much to Julia's surprise, he wore a modest pair of navy boxer shorts.

Soon Doreen lay face down on the couch, presenting her flaccid buttocks and flabby thighs for Grant's ministrations. She could do with a tone-up in the gym, Julia thought. Remembering the well-honed body of Tanya Wentworth, who worked out twice a week, she concluded that it was hardly surprising Jeremy preferred to make love with his mistress.

As the massage proceeded, however, Julia was aware that Grant was using a different approach from before. His touch seemed less lingering, resembling more the clinical thoroughness of the physiotherapist than the sensual caress of the lover. And Mrs Cadstock was certainly not getting sexually aroused. She lay sprawled and comatose like a fat, contented cat. Even when she turned over and Grant reached the erogenous zones of her thighs and stomach she showed no signs of finding the massage titillating, only relaxing.

'My God, I do believe he's giving her a straight massage!' Julia gasped aloud.

It was true. Moving up from her plump belly to her large breasts Grant began to knead them with neutral efficiency, avoiding the nipples entirely, while Doreen lay in a trance-like state of well-being. He moved on to her arms and hands, then her face and scalp, ending with an all-over cologne rub. After that he went to wash his hands and Julia knew that the session must be over.

She was left feeling deeply puzzled. It was true that a few members of *Sybarites* used it as a straight health club, but when Julia had interviewed Doreen she'd formed the distinct impression that she was looking forward to the same treatment that her 'friend' Tanya so enjoyed. Once again she wondered whether Doreen knew about Tanya's affair with her husband. Could the two women possibly be complicit, in some way?

Doreen re-appeared from the cubicle, wearing her blue jersey dress and carrying her raincoat and bag. She began talking to Grant in quite an animated way and he was answering her at length. Julia wished she could eavesdrop. Perhaps they were reminiscing about the cruise they'd both been on, Doreen as a passenger and Grant as a crew member. Yes, that must be it. They might even be friends. To her surprise Julia found that, where Grant's relations with other women was concerned, intimate conversation made her just as envious as physical intimacy. But her status as his employer inevitably placed a barrier between them, and one which Julia would overstep at her peril. With a sigh she realised that polite chit-chat was the most she could expect to exchange with Grant in future.

To Julia's surprise, the massage session ended with them shaking hands. Doreen's exit was accompanied by a click from the video, and Julia realised that the tape had run out. As she waited for it to rewind she remembered that it contained film not only of Grant massaging Doreen, Rebecca and Lou, but also of her own session with him. A deep, secret thrill went through her, similar to the buzz she got when she thought about the collection of sex toys in her private sauna. This tape was special. When it had rewound Julia slipped it from the machine and into her leather handbag.

For the rest of the day Julia kept herself busy drafting a contract for the solar heating company, ordering new equipment and going through her accounts. She was sick of thinking about Grant

Delaney, and coping with the knots of frustrated desire that formed in her stomach whenever she remembered the deep satisfaction he'd given her. At the end of the afternoon Julia felt like using her sauna, but resisted the urge. She knew what would happen, and if she was trying to put Grant out of her mind that was definitely not the way to do it.

Once she was home, however, in the privacy of her penthouse flat, Julia felt the old itch return. She took a shower and washed her hair, then put on the video and lounged on the soft leather sofa in her silk kimono while she flicked the remote control. The first sight of herself with Grant made her gasp aloud. They were standing close together, Julia with her hand on the massage couch and the masseur just in front, listening attentively while she explained about the aromatherapy oils. Even the most impartial observer would have to admit that they made an attractive couple, but there was more to it than that. Their body language spoke volumes. Julia almost blushed as she saw herself smiling coyly and unconsciously drawing attention to her eyes and mouth with little, fluttery movements. It was exactly the sort of behaviour she despised in other women. Furthermore she was mirroring Grant's posture, with her legs apart, head to one side. They were surveying each other like a pair of animals preparing to mate, and Julia couldn't help noticing that Grant's gaze was taking in every contour of her body even before she took off her clothes. She put the video into slow motion and their movements took on the aspect of a graceful and erotic ballet as they shifted posture, gestured, moved about the room in perfect harmony with each other.

After Julia had disappeared into the changing cubicle, Grant wiped a hand briefly across his brow in a telling gesture, then began to strip too. He had his back to the camera, but as he lifted his right leg to get out of his boxer shorts Julia could see the heavy, dark sac swinging between his thighs. She could almost feel the ripe heaviness of his balls in her palm. 'Oh God!' she murmured, restlessly crossing then uncrossing her legs. She saw herself emerge from the cubicle while Grant was trying to squeeze his equipment into the inadequate G-string and noted the widening of her pupils as she glimpsed his glans, just poking over the top. From her viewing position on the sofa, Julia giggled. She froze the video at the point where the camera had the best shot and gazed her fill, feeling deliciously guilty and schoolgirlish. What would Grant think if he knew she'd been ogling him? The thought sobered her up a little, but didn't diminish the slow tide of desire that had been building in her all day. As she let the film continue, Julia opened her gown and began to caress her already firm breasts, sighing as the familiar currents began swirling through her erogenous zones.

Now he was smoothing the warm oil over her buttocks, an expression of dreamy concentration on his handsome face as his eyes followed his fingers into the dark cleft. Julia could remember exactly how his hands had felt, how subtle, yet how sure. It had been as if he knew her body of old, as if they'd been lovers for years and her flesh was as familiar to him as his own. She watched him travel up and down her spine, this time experiencing the rhythm of the massage through his hands rather than through her own skin. Seeing him at work she could imagine how determined he had been to do a good job, to give her pleasure. His skill and dedication delighted her. It was like watching a sensitive and passionate musician playing, coaxing the full range

51

of responses from the delicate instrument of her body.

She turned over, at his bidding, and he started massaging her toes. Julia could now see him eyeing the matted vee that concealed her sex while he worked. His mouth was slightly open and a bead of sweat was trickling over his upper lip. Julia could almost smell again the musky scent of him, mingled with the sweeter aroma of ylang-ylang. She could certainly feel a tingling in her toes, which were responding keenly to the sight of Grant rubbing them on-screen.

As he came slowly up her legs, past her knees, to knead her thighs Julia could see that he was fully erect. There was no mistaking it: she could see the entire length of his prick clearly outlined beneath the pouch, with the dusky pink helmet peeking over the top. She felt an urgent shudder in her womb at the realisation that he had been as aroused as she'd been by the massage. At the time she had been somewhat disconcerted when he seemed to change tack, temporarily abandoning her lower half to concentrate on her face. Now Julia realised that it had been for his own benefit, an attempt to calm himself down so he could remain in control.

'He fancied me! He really wanted me!' she breathed aloud. There was a kind of relief in realising what she had always known at some subliminal level, but hardly dared to believe. The guy had been so turned on by the sight of her sex that he'd had to change to a more neutral area to dampen down his lust. Julia chuckled, rubbing her warm stomach in sensual glee and murmuring, 'Oh yes, Grant Delaney, the attraction was mutual all right! My candid camera reveals all!'

She watched in fascination, her heart throbbing with excitement, as he came at last to stand between her outstretched legs in the space made by the divided couch. Once he got to work on her in earnest it was impossible for Julia to remain a detached observer. Her hand crept to her crotch and she mimicked his actions, writhing on the sofa just as she was squirming on the couch, returning to that dark realm of the senses where he had so expertly taken her.

Except now she was seeing it from his perspective, watching his mouth sucking at her while he rubbed her clitoris with his finger and plainly becoming excited again himself. When he squatted beneath her thighs she saw him release his straining tool from the ridiculous little black bag. Now it stood straight up, a beautiful tawny stem with a pink, bulbous head. Julia felt her vagina convulse at the sight and a surge of pure joy traversed her body from end to end. She had only seen a few naked pricks before. Two or three under-developed adolescent ones followed by one brief glimpse of her first, short-lived boyfriend's, and finally Leo's. She had certainly never thought of the male organ as a thing of beauty before, and yet now she was entranced by the sight of this magnificent specimen, so long and thick and smooth, raising its delicate head as if longing to gain access to her own damply inviting nest, just above it. There was a kind of poignant poetry about it, as if her sex and his were a pair of thwarted lovers kept apart by some twist of fate or petty social taboo. Everything about the scene suggested that they should be gloriously united, and yet Julia knew that they would not be. It was almost unbearable to watch such a spectacle of unfulfilled desire.

It was already obvious that Grant was finding it pretty unbearable too. By the time Julia was on the slow exquisite climb towards her earth-shattering orgasm, and quite incapable of noticing anything going on around her, Grant had evidently decided that his need was as urgent as hers. While he licked and sucked her to a climax, using one hand to help her along, he was using his other hand to help himself. Julia watched, bleary-eyed, as he grasped his shaft and began to rub vigorously. She saw the end swell and yield a single dewy drop. Then, as she thrashed and moaned in the throes of her own ecstasy, Grant's hand moved faster, his face became suddenly contorted with extreme emotion and there was a spurt of white juice from the pulsating head of his penis.

The sight of the arcing spray, accompanied by her own expressions of ultimate pleasure, led Julia to thrust her fingers deep inside her. She was almost on the point of coming and, with a few deft circlings of her wrist against the hard nub of her clitoris, she orgasmed in a series of shattering convulsions that left her limp and spent. The video played on: dimly she was aware of Grant making an effort to recover his cool, first cleaning up her sodden pubic area then wiping his hands on a paper towel. And she'd thought he was just removing the massage oil! Even when he turned to wash his hands at the basin she could see that he was shaken, visibly trembling.

Once she had disappeared into the shower, Grant doused his head and chest with cold water in a determined attempt to return to normality. But when he turned and faced the camera for a few seconds his face said it all. He had found the experience just as cataclysmic as she had, but would die rather than admit it. Seeing his expression, caught so ambivalently between vulnerability and bravado, Julia felt a surprising tenderness and compassion. She wished she'd been able to take him in her arms, to tell him it was all right, that she understood how sexual passion could turn macho men into weaklings and feeble women into heroines. But what had she done? Turned her back on him abruptly, to hide her own feelings, and taken a shower.

Yet how could it have been otherwise? Their professional code had required each to hide their true feelings from the other. Just minutes later they had confronted each other over an office desk as if nothing more exciting than a handshake had just occurred between them. They had pretended to be perfectly normal, even talking about the massage as if it had been a routine exercise instead of a passionate encounter. What brilliant actors they both were!

The phone rang, startling Julia out of her reflections. At once she sprang from the sofa, half convinced that the call must be from Grant. So when Leo's deep, urbane voice greeted her she felt her whole body sag with disappointment.

'Hullo, Leo. How are you?'

'Fine. How's business?'

'We're doing very well.' Julia couldn't help a note of satisfied triumph creeping into her tone as she continued, 'Membership is well up on last month and we've almost covered the bank loan. It won't be long before the new wing has paid for itself.'

Leo had warned her about not expanding too fast, suggesting that membership was probably near capacity. 'After all,' she recalled him saying, 'how many frustrated women can one town hold?'

'Quite a few,' she'd felt like saying, 'if all the men are like you.' Yet she had always shrunk from confronting him, always colluded with Leo to protect his precious, inflated ego.

'Jolly good,' he said now, distantly. 'Well I hope things continue to go well for you, but actually I'm ringing up to give you a bit of a warning.'

'Oh?'

'You probably saw today's *Gazette* . . .'

'Yes. Our beloved MP . . .'

'The very same. High moral tone, and all that. I expect you were hoping it was all hot air, but I have it on good information through the grapevine that he's planning a clean-up of his own back yard, if you follow me.'

Julia felt chilled. She wrapped the thin silk more tightly across her chest, trying to sound unconcerned. 'Was he still talking in general terms, or was he more specific?'

'There was mention of "massage parlours" I believe, amongst other things, but I shouldn't worry yourself unduly. You have a licence from the council as a health club. Anyone visiting the premises can see that there's a pool, gym, sauna and so on. What goes on between your masseurs and their clients is strictly confidential, isn't it? So I shouldn't worry. But you might want to vet prospective members a bit more carefully. You wouldn't want any snoopers getting in there, now would you, telling tales out of school?'

'No, of course not. But I always check references . . .'

'Quite so. Well, that was all I was ringing for. We must get together for a drink sometime soon. 'Bye for now.'

Julia put down the phone feeling cross. Why did he still have to patronise her, even though their marriage was over? Sometimes she wished she'd moved away from that town altogether, started a new life somewhere else, but giving up *Sybarites* would have been too much of a sacrifice. When Leo briefly invaded her life from time to time it brought out all the old resentments in her. Still, it was a salutary reminder that she had, indeed, made the right decision in divorcing him.

That night Julia found it hard to get to sleep. The three men who were causing her concern – Grant, Leo, Jeremy Cadstock – all seemed to be caught up in some web of intrigue relating to *Sybarites*, and the factor that linked them was sex. Not normally one to indulge in paranoid fantasies, Julia recognised that this time she was hardly an impartial observer. Her own sexuality was part of the equation, along with her business. Put the two together, and her entire life was on the line. But what to do about it?

For the moment all she could do was sit tight, be vigilant, and wait for developments. The *Sybarites* licence wasn't up for renewal for another three months and hopefully the whole Cadstock campaign would fizzle out by then, or get channelled into drafting some bill that would have to take its chances with all the other proposed legislation.

As for keeping her licence, Julia knew she had enough friends on the council. She mused once again, as she had at the beginning, on the advantages of the system. Her club was a boon to those whose wives regularly gained their satisfaction there, leaving their husbands free to enjoy their 'bit on the side'. It was an arrangement that some wives had enjoyed for generations, although when men consorted with prostitutes there was always the risk of them bringing disease back to the marital bed.

At *Sybarites*, however, there was no risk. Women could be thoroughly satisfied with no danger to their health. On the contrary, they often left the club looking radiant and, in some cases, years younger. They had the choice of ten virile, attractive young men to pleasure them and the arrangement gave them all the benefits of an affair with none of the dangers.

There was one potential flaw in the arrangement: what if one of the women became infatuated with a masseur and started pestering him? This had worried Julia at the beginning but, in fact, it had never happened. Any member was free to book the same man every day if she wished but, since the masseurs were thoroughly professional and their contact with their clients purely physical, complications were unlikely to occur. It gave the lie to the theory that women needed to feel emotionally involved to enjoy sex. They were emotionally involved with their husbands or boyfriends, but sometimes their partner could not meet their sexual needs, for whatever reason, and finding another man to relieve them put less strain on their primary relationship. The more Julia saw how fulfilled the women looked, and how much happier their marriages often became, the more convinced she was that *Sybarites* was performing a valuable social service.

When she examined her position coolly Julia was reassured that she had little to fear from Jeremy Cadstock or anyone else. Her personal life was another matter. Leo's phone call had reminded her that he could still pull her strings, still make her feel insecure, however temporarily. Then there was Grant. How ironic that while the club members had resisted the charms of their masseur, the club owner herself had succumbed. Julia sighed. Perhaps she had tried to be too self-sufficient. If there had been another man in her life maybe she wouldn't have over-reacted to Grant. Because that was all it was, an over-reaction.

Yet as she turned once again into a more comfortable sleeping position Julia could feel her empty vagina aching, like a barren womb, for what it could never have.

Chapter Five

JULIA HAD WORKED really hard all day. She'd enrolled three new members – two of them nominated by Rebecca and Lou – seen Phil, her accountant, had lunch with the editor of *Healthy Life* magazine who wanted to feature *Sybarites* in an article on women's health clubs, accompanied the photographer while he took photos for the new brochure and spent the last part of the afternoon talking to a very keen young man who wanted her to switch to a chlorine-free method of aerating the pool. After a quick evening meal at the Healthfood Bar, Julia returned to her office and drafted some notes for her interview with the *Healthy Life* reporter next week.

All of which had kept her mind off the three men who currently filled her with various kinds of disquiet: Jeremy, Leo and Grant. She hadn't seen Grant at all, either on video or in the flesh, and began to hope that the dangerous effect he had on her was beginning to diminish. 'Out of sight, out of mind', that was the principle she was working on. And, so far, it did seem to be working.

It was almost ten p.m. by the time Julia stretched in her office chair and decided to call it a day and a half. She thought of relaxing in her sauna but then changed her mind. The club closed at ten and then she could have the main pool all to herself. It would be a chance to think about what the aeration man had said, to test the quality of the water and decide whether it could be improved upon. Yes, she would take a swim.

Ben, the evening receptionist, was just leaving when Julia crossed the foyer on her way to the pool.

'Everyone else gone home, Ben?' she called.

'Almost everyone. One or two of the masseurs might still be here. And Jim, of course.'

Julia nodded. Jim Thomson, the caretaker, was one of her most loyal and thorough workers. He never left the premises until he'd made his rounds, which included almost everywhere from the boiler room to the broom cupboards. The only exceptions were the two rooms leading off Julia's office which she cleaned herself, and kept locked whenever she wasn't there.

'Okay. I'm just going to cool off in the pool. Good night, Ben.'

'Goodnight, Miss Julia. Enjoy your swim.'

The pool looked beautiful in the evening light, the turquoise water completely still and clear. Julia had put a lot of thought into its refurbishment. When Leo had run the place the 'greenery' was all plastic and the décor functional in appearance. Inspired by the baths of ancient Rome, Julia had transformed the walls with erotic murals along the lines of Pompeii, placed a fountain in a niche between two columns at one end and let it play on to musical chimes, so that the air was filled with tinkling harmony instead of the crude pop tunes that Leo had insisted were what the members wanted.

'You can't get away from that irritating noise these days,' she'd told him, sure of her ground.

'Shops, pubs, stations, everywhere. I want to create an atmosphere of calm and relaxation around the pool.'

She had certainly succeeded. Extending her credit with the bank, Julia had insisted on installing real plants that were supplied and cared for by a local firm. In the warm, steamy atmosphere tropical palms, vines and creepers flourished, lending an exotic air to the environment. Despite Leo's caustic suggestion that she should import live parrots and maybe a few snakes, the whole concept worked really well.

Julia stripped off at the side of the pool, leaving her clothes neatly folded on one of several padded leather couches, ranged as if for a Roman orgy. There was the scent of roses in the air. Looking down for a moment at the unruffled, virginal surface of the water she felt a thrill of warm anticipation. She dived smoothly in, feeling the silken caress of the water against her naked skin as she went under then re-surfaced.

Swimming at a leisurely pace, Julia did several lengths in different styles. She had always been a strong swimmer and loved the water. When she was lying on her back, using just her legs to propel her gently towards the far end, the door to the pool suddenly swung open.

Julia saw at once that it was Grant. He stood on the side for a few seconds watching her, his mouth half smiling, his eyes the same colour as the water. Then he called, softly, 'Hi, Julia. I hope I'm not disturbing you. Would you mind if I joined you? I'll go away again if you'd rather be by yourself.'

She knew what she *should* say. Somehow, though, different words came out.

'No, do stay Grant. Come on in, the water's lovely!'

He grinned, squatting and bending his dark head to untie his trainers. Julia swam back breast-stroke, watching him all the way. Having resolutely avoided thinking about him all day, to see him before her now was a kind of shock. When he stripped off his shirt and revealed his well-moulded chest it was all she could do to smother a sigh of longing. He turned his back on her while he took off his trousers, but when he got out of his pants and presented her with a pair of firm, dimpled buttocks she felt she would drown in her own molten desire.

Vividly the memory of what she'd seen on the video returned, reminding her of how his penis looked when aroused. Grant turned suddenly and caught her looking at it and she immediately plunged below the water to hide her embarrassment. As she surfaced she was aware that he'd taken the plunge too, and they both rose up laughing, face to face.

With his black hair dampened down like the shiny pelt of a sea lion, drops clinging to his dark lashes and rivulets creeping down between the matted hairs of his chest, Grant exuded a raw magnetism that held Julia entranced. She saw his eyes drop to her torso as they stood in the shallows, aware that her nipples were puckered and her breasts jutting firmly. He looked as if he might reach out and touch them. Julia held her breath, willing him, against all reason, to make that one advance. If he did, she knew they would soon be kissing and caressing above and below the water then, maybe, migrating on to one of the couches to finish off what they'd begun. She wanted it – oh, how she wanted it! And she sensed that he did too.

So when he threw her a boyish grin and said, 'Race you to the other end!' Julia felt disappointment grip like a manacle round her heart.

'Okay.'

He gave her a short headstart but still outswam her by a length or so. Nevertheless, he was gracious in victory. 'You're a good swimmer – for a woman. Ever done any training?'

Julia grasped the rail and swung round to face him. 'As a teenager I swam for my school, but I don't really like being competitive. These days, I prefer to relax rather than push myself.'

'Saving the competitive instinct for business, is that it?'

'Something like that.'

She moved away from him, drifting towards the steps that led towards the spa whirlpool. 'I think I'll take a break right now. It's been a long day.'

As Julia rose from the water to climb the steps she was aware of Grant's eyes on her. Was he thinking about how it had felt to knead her buttocks, stroke her thighs? The very thought made her go weak at the knees and stumble on the slippery steps.

'I'll do a few more lengths,' Grant called. She turned to watch his powerful shoulders cleave the water for a few strokes, then descended into the limpid peace of the whirlpool.

Julia was pleased with the design of the spa bath, which was tessellated like a Roman pavement and had a mosaic picture of a dolphin on the floor. There was a button at the side which controlled the speed of the bubbles. Julia set it to low, which gave her a gentle massage all over, like bathing in warm champagne. She sat on the underwater ridge which served as a seat and put her head back with a sigh. But the presence of Grant in the pool next door made it impossible for her to relax completely. Over the gentle fizzing of the whirlpool she could hear him rhythmically breaking the surface of the water as he swam length after length in an easy crawl.

Whatever had possessed her to let him stay? She

was in charge, she could have told him, Garbo fashion, that she wanted to be alone. She could have felt safe, had a proper rest. Now his presence kept her on edge, even amongst the soothing effervescence that normally had such a calming effect on her. Well perhaps he would stay in the main pool and leave her alone.

No chance. She heard him approach the steps with a few strong strokes and then he loomed above her, amongst the palms. 'Me Tarzan, you Jane?' he grinned, his arm around a tough hanging vine. 'Or shall we play at Adam and Eve?'

Julia couldn't help glancing at the long, dusky phallus hanging between those strong wet thighs. Huskily she replied, 'Caesar and Cleopatra would be more in keeping with the style I was aiming at.'

He began to descend the steps, slowly. 'Are you casting me in the Rex Harrison part? I'd prefer Mark Antony. So much more romantic to play Burton to your Taylor, don't you think?'

'I'm flattered. But how come you know the cast of *Cleopatra* so well? Don't tell me you're a movie buff.'

He grinned modestly as he glided across the pool to sit beside her. 'A bit of one. My Dad ran a cinema so I got to know most of the classic films.'

'Really?' Julia realised how little she knew about him, this man who had brought her more intense satisfaction than any other. She shifted lazily in the water, aware of how easily his outstretched legs might entwine with hers in the blue deep. Part of her wanted to continue their conversation, but another part wanted just to feel his presence, along with the gentle massaging bubbles, to drift away on a sensual dream of what might have been. Julia closed her eyes and floated in blissful peace for a few seconds.

Suddenly the pace of the whirlpool quickened,

the water boiled and fizzed as the jets sent out a faster stream. Julia's eyes flicked open and she sat up. Grant's blue eyes were smiling apologetically at her.

'I pressed the button – do you mind? I need a bit of a shoulder massage.'

'No, I don't mind.'

Julia closed her eyes again and tried to resume her former floating position but she was tossed this way and that by the slipstream. She found herself riding on a current, feeling a strong jet play between her thighs, another spray her breasts. Beside her, just an arm's length away, Grant also lay in the midst of swirling water, his shoulders braced low against the side and his toes peeping up from the water in front of him.

'Mm, so good!' he murmured.

There was a persistent upsurge of water forcing Julia's legs apart. At first she tried to change position but then she gave in, feeling the powerful stream gush against her sex, making the delicate tissues tingle with unexpected pleasure. She shifted very slightly and the water played directly on to her erect clitoris. For a few seconds it was uncomfortable until she got the angle right, then the familiar warm throbbing began.

'This is madness!' she told herself. With Grant so near it would be almost impossible for her to hide her arousal. And yet it was incredibly exciting to think of it all going on under water without him realising. Or did he realise? She gave him a sidelong glance but he seemed absorbed in his own hydrotherapy treatment. Julia let her eyes roam unchecked over every square inch of him that was exposed: the handsome profile – not unlike that of the Roman statue in the alcove – broad shoulders and strong neck, leading down to his wonderfully muscled chest streaked with wet-blackened hairs.

'Oh!' she gave an involuntary gasp as an intruding stream of bubbles found its way between her slack labia and into her vagina. The effect was like a douche and, coupled with the continuous erotic play on her clitoris, propelled her to the verge of an orgasm.

'What's the matter?' Grant asked, his eyes opening lazily.

Julia did her best to sound normal. 'Nothing. I just lost my balance, that's all.'

'I could turn it down again, if you'd rather.'

'No!' Julia knew she was at the point of no return and her voice came out jerkily. 'No, it's okay, really.'

He closed his eyes again and she felt safe to let the stimulating water play continue. It was easy to imagine him reaching out with his strong hand and opening her up, fingering the soft petals of her sex, rubbing the hard concealed bud just the way she liked it. Julia trembled at the thought that it might be Grant's hard penis, not the fierce aquajet, playing at her entrance, his lips nudging at her breasts and washing her nipples with cool saliva. She wriggled, tilting her pelvis as if to allow him entrance, and suddenly the tide was flowing both ways as the spurt from the pool met the pressure of her pulsating sex. Julia was caught in the maelstrom and it was Grant's face she saw as she gave herself up to the exquisite sensations, Grant who was penetrating the psychic core of her being just as surely as the water jet was invading her physical centre.

Unable to censor herself, Julia moaned softly as the lovely ripples died. She opened her eyes and saw Grant staring at her with an expression of faint amusement.

'Oh, I must have been dreaming!' she muttered, colouring. 'I think I'll take a swim now.'

She moved quickly to the steps but he was just

behind. 'I'll come too'.

The main pool felt safer than the warm intimacy of the whirlpool. Julia forced her unwilling legs into action and swam a few slow lengths while Grant soon overtook her, moving with swift grace. When the warm thrill within her had completely subsided and she felt almost normal – as normal as she could feel while she and Grant were bathing in the same element – Julia waited for him in the shallows, crouching so that her bosom lay just below the waterline.

He came up to the rail, stopped and grinned. 'Had enough?'

'I ought to be getting home.'

'So should I. But I haven't had so much fun for ages. This is the first time I've got to use the pool.'

Julia heard herself slip into her 'business' voice. 'Well all the masseurs are welcome to use the pool any time after hours . . .'

Suddenly Grant dived beneath her and pulled her off her feet. She screamed and he laughed, blowing bubbles underwater. He splashed her as he came to the surface, then began to circle round her flicking water at her. She flicked back, then scooped up two handfuls and threw it at him, dousing his head. For several minutes they frisked like playful dolphins in the shallows until Julia finally clambered out, giggling, and went for her towel.

While she dried herself Grant swam another couple of lengths. She watched his powerful back and shoulders rising and falling in the aquamarine pool, and a fierce wave of longing went through her. If only she dared ask him to give her a massage, now, while they were alone in the building. Her skin, already tingling from the whirlpool, prickled all over at the thought of his touch and the pulse deep inside her began its slow, steady throb. If only she dared . . .

Grant was getting out of the pool, pulling himself up on to the side with his strong arms, reaching for the thick white towel he'd brought from the massage room.

'I've worked up quite a thirst,' he said, looking frankly at Julia while she picked up her bra. 'Have to get a juice out of the machine, or something.'

'We can have a drink in the Healthfood Bar if you like, I have the keys.' Julia paused, summoning her courage. 'Then, if you're not in a hurry . . .'

The door to the pool opened with a thud and Jim Thomson, the caretaker, appeared.

'Oh, I beg your pardon Miss Julia. I had no idea you were still here.'

'That's quite all right, Jim. We're going soon.'

The interruption had been timely. Julia had forgotten that they were not the only ones left in the building. A massage was out of the question now. She was filled with an odd mixture of disappointment and relief.

She dressed quickly, then led the way from the pool to the Healthfood Bar down the corridor. She went behind the counter and asked what Grant wanted. He chose a tropical cocktail of pineapple, orange and guava juice. She gave it to him in a long glass with a straw, then made one for herself. Soon they were sitting companionably side by side at one of the white tables, and Julia began to feel at ease again.

'So, Grant, how are you settling in?'

He eyed her over his stripey straw. 'Okay, I think. Perhaps you should ask my clients.'

'You've only had a few so far, haven't you? Doreen Cadstock, for instance.'

She regarded him closely for any sign of reaction but his expression remained pleasantly impassive.

'Doreen, yes. I've massaged her before, you

68

know, when we were on the Good Ship Lollipop.'

'On the *what*?'

He grinned. 'That was what we used to call it. It was our little joke. You know, after the Shirley Temple song? The ship's real name was the *Lilliput*. As cruise vessels go she was rather small, so the passengers and crew got to know each other quite well.'

'I'll bet!'

Julia regretted the coarse innuendo as soon as it had passed her lips. It revealed what she already knew, that she was envious of the casual intimacy that seemed to exist between Grant and Doreen. He raised his eyebrows but said nothing so Julia continued, nervously, 'Not that anyone could accuse you of unprofessional conduct, I'm sure. In fact, two of your other clients, Rebecca and Lou, must have been satisfied because they've recruited a couple more members.'

If she expected him to give anything away, Julia was disappointed. His face showed ordinary pleasure, that was all. 'Really? That's good. They said they would recommend me . . . I mean the club, to all their friends.'

'That's the spirit. If we go on like this we shall reach capacity soon.'

Grant put down his glass, giving Julia a straight look. 'I'm very impressed by what you've got going here, Julia. I worked in several health clubs before I went on the cruise ships, and this is the best run establishment I've seen. Somehow you've managed to achieve a totally non-sleazy atmosphere. The place has real class.'

'I believe a health club is only as good as its staff,' she smiled, gratified nevertheless. 'You can have all the equipment and facilities in the world and still fall down on service.'

'Well you've certainly succeeded here. It's the kind of place I wouldn't be ashamed to bring my own mother to.'

His *mother*? Julia smothered a giggle and, with it, her curiosity about what kind of a person that lady might be. Instead, she made the conversation take a more serious turn.

'Even so, there are people who would like to see us closed down.'

Grant looked startled. 'Surely not!'

'Oh yes! Not everyone is as enlightened about female sexual needs as you and me, Grant. That's why I have to keep what goes on here strictly confidential. If the truth leaked out there are certain crusading moralists who would campaign to have us closed down.'

That was as far as she dared go. If Grant recognised the oblique reference he didn't show it. Instead, pushing back his chair, he rose to his feet. 'Time to go. Thanks for letting me share your evening swim, Julia. It was great.'

Julia rose too. 'That's okay.' She sought an excuse to prolong the evening, but found none. 'Well . . . er . . . I'd better tell Jim we're going so he can lock up.'

They said goodnight and went their different ways, Grant through the main door and Julia back towards the pool where she'd last seen the caretaker. She still had the wild hope in her heart that, if she hurried, she might meet Grant in the car park and he would be unable to let her go home alone. Julia knew he was attracted to her. That evening every look, every word, every casual touch had charged with an undercurrent of sexual tension that she would have found totally unbearable if she had not discharged some of it in the spa pool. Would he, in his turn, go home and masturbate while thinking of her? The thought stirred new eddies of desire in her, which she tried in vain to quash.

Jim was in the boiler room but by the time she found him Julia had heard Grant's car drive off into the night. She left herself, soon after, but was not looking forward to what remained of the evening. Arriving home at half past eleven she switched on the television and poured herself a generous measure of Southern Comfort. Finding it impossible to concentrate on the late-night chat show she took a shower and was about to go to bed when she noticed there was a message on the answerphone. No doubt it had been left while she was in the bathroom.

Julia pressed the switch and was amazed to hear Grant's voice.

'Hullo, Julia, it's Grant. I just wanted to thank you for helping me settle in so easily. I thought it would be hard settling down to a shore job, but I feel like I've been at *Sybarites* for months already. Well, that's all. See you tomorrow!'

The message left her with a warm glow. He was such fun to be with, the kind of man who appealed to women of all ages, with whom women felt comfortable. When they were alone together it was so easy to forget her authority over him. Perhaps they could be more like friends, after all.

Then Julia remembered how she'd felt at the pool, just being near him, and it was like cold water in her face. Who was she trying to kid? She didn't just want to be friends with Grant, she wanted them to be lovers. And that would never do. It would never do at all.

Chapter Six

SLEEP WAS BECOMING a problem. Even if Julia managed to fall asleep fairly quickly she would wake early. Then, instead of lying in bed and allowing herself to dwell on thoughts of the men in her life, past and present, she would get up. After doing her yoga, she would prepare herself a healthy breakfast of muesli, fruit and herb tea, then settle down for the bland chit-chat of the TV programme *Morning Call*.

The day after her swim with Grant, Julia was up at six-thirty and being bored by the vacuous blonde presenter, Lindsay King, harping on about nothing in particular. Suddenly, though, she was startled to hear Jeremy Cadstock's name mentioned.

'. . . here in the studio to answer some questions about his "Common Decency" campaign,' Lindsay continued, smiling. The camera panned to show the MP sitting in an armchair and sipping orange juice.

'Now then, Jeremy, you seem to have caused quite a stir with your plan to clean up Britain. First, would you tell us more about your aims?'

'Certainly, Lindsay.' Jeremy smiled, unctuously, his grey eyes alight with evangelical zeal. 'I'd like to remind you that, as a democratically elected MP, I sit in the House of *Commons* as a representative of the *common* people. Now the term "common decency" means what ordinary people consider to be decent, and I think there's general agreement about this. Most people know what is decent and proper, and they don't want to be bombarded with the kind of filth that passes for entertainment these days.'

'What exactly are you referring to, Jeremy?'

'Pornographic magazines and videos, for a start. No clean-living citizen wants these on display in shops where children can see them. Most of us would rather they were not produced at all, but if we must have them let them at least go back under the counter where they belong.'

'So you're only concerned about the possible corruption of children, are you?'

'Not at all. Take television, for example. Since we've had this "nine o'clock watershed" nonsense it's given producers licence to put on all sorts of disgusting programmes later in the evening.'

'I see. So you're trying to bring stricter censorship into the media in general.'

'Yes, but that's not the whole story.' He brushed a lock of his grey, thinning hair back into position and leaned forward, earnestly. 'I want this government to do away with the menace of dirty phone lines, sex shops and all so-called "massage parlours" and "health clubs" that are little more than brothels.'

Lindsay looked sceptical. 'Are you saying that you're trying to do away with prostitution altogether?'

'In a perfect world that would be the ideal. But I'm a bit more down to earth than that, Lindsay. I recognise that we're not going to get rid of the oldest profession entirely, so what I would like to see is state licensed and controlled brothels. It's a system that works well in some other countries.'

73

'Your proposals are very wide-ranging, aren't they?'

'Yes, but unfortunately the problem has become a widespread and complex one to which there's no single solution. Obviously the drafting of the bill will take some considerable thought, but I'm hoping to present it to Parliament before the end of this session.'

'Well good luck, Jeremy. I've a feeling you're going to need it. And thank you very much for coming in to talk to us this morning.'

Julia turned off the TV then sat back on her sofa feeling as if someone had punched her in the stomach. That man was dangerous. He had the burning light of conviction in his eye and a will to succeed that was frightening. If the 'common decency' idea really took hold there would be no stopping him. The time was ripe for a puritanical backlash. Society already regretted its lost innocence, and anyone who persuaded the public that it could be magically restored was on a winning ticket.

Yet how could a man like Cadstock prate of morality when he was deceiving his wife with another woman? Could the rumours of their affair be unfounded? But the pair had been seen boarding a plane to Paris together and, on another occasion, they had been spotted in an out-of-the-way country hotel ogling each other over breakfast. There were many people who made it their business to know what prominent citizens like Cadstock got up to, and Julia knew the information came from reliable sources. One of them was a police inspector friend of Leo's.

It was angering to think that the likes of Jeremy Cadstock believed they could get away with it but, unless they put a foot wrong elsewhere, they generally did. Hypocrisy was not a vice despised by the ruling party – indeed, they thrived on it. Not even moral crusaders had to be squeaky clean in all areas, and to have a mistress was seldom regarded as a crime unless there was a security leak or the unfortunate birth of a love-child. In targeting prostitution and pornography, Jeremy was not invading the thorny territory of private morals, only public ones.

Still, Julia thought as she prepared to leave, it would do no harm to keep a video record of all visits to the club made by Doreen and Tanya. You never knew when such evidence might come in handy.

As fate would have it, Julia saw Tanya Wentworth at the club's reception desk as soon as she arrived that morning.

'Yes, your massage is booked with Grant for ten o'clock,' Steven was confirming as Julia strode towards them.

'Hullo Tanya,' she beamed, trying to appear casual. 'Change of masseur today?'

The woman turned with a smile. Julia was always impressed by her extraordinary looks: the deep auburn hair that framed her heart-shaped face in a rich, thick curtain, the mouth that seemed far too full and sensual for so delicate a face and the large, emerald eyes that flashed sultry elemental fire at men and women alike. Today a simple blue and white frock understated the curves of her impressive figure, hinting provocatively at what lay beneath. Tanya nodded. 'I'm normally happy with Marlon, as you know, but Doreen recommended Grant so I thought I'd give him a try for a change. He's new here, isn't he?'

'Yes. Actually, it was Doreen who recommended him to me. I gather they knew each other from some cruise ship.'

'Ah yes! Doreen went on a Mediterranean cruise last winter.'

'I'm surprised her husband found the time . . .'

Tanya gave a tinkling laugh. 'Oh, she went by herself! She'd been ill and Jeremy suggested it would be a nice way to convalesce. Doreen was a bit apprehensive at first, but everyone made her welcome and she had a lovely holiday.'

Julia thought, 'While the cat's away . . .' She gave Tanya a cool smile. 'Anyway, I hope you find Grant satisfactory. We've had no complaints so far.'

Tanya moved off towards the gym. Turning back to discuss the business of the day with Steve, Julia felt a strange excitement creep through her. She had the feeling that some kind of intrigue was being played out between Tanya, Doreen and Grant. Well, if anything untoward went on during this morning's sessions she would have it on tape.

Julia was too busy to watch the massage as it happened. She had a meeting with the photographer to select the shots for the new brochure, then she was interviewing a prospective member. At lunch-time, though, she brought a sandwich and a fruit juice into her viewing room and switched on the tape of Tanya's session.

While she waited for the woman to emerge from the changing cubicle, Julia felt a knot of tension form at the base of her stomach. Part of her believed that if she watched Grant massaging other women, many other women, he would lose the special attraction he seemed to have for her. She would come to accept that what he had done for her had, from his point of view at least, been merely routine.

Another part of her was both excited and dismayed by her spying activities. There was no doubt that seeing other women being pleasured by hunky males turned her on, but she found it hard to accept her role of voyeur. Now that she had admitted to herself how much she wanted Grant, it was difficult to pretend that her viewing sessions were for security purposes only.

Well, it couldn't go on for much longer. Already Grant's workload had increased and soon Julia wouldn't have time to watch him with all his clients.

On screen, Tanya appeared loosely draped in a white towel which she casually discarded onto a chair. Although she worked out it was only to keep the body nature had endowed her with in the peak of condition, with no exaggerated musculature. Julia watched as Grant's blue eyes quickly took in the detail of her torso. Her biceps were visible but not hefty, her pecs were firm but not overdeveloped like some women, where the breasts were mere appendages of the muscle. Tanya's breasts were perfectly round and firm, standing out proud from her ribcage above her flat stomach. Julia noticed Grant's look of surprise as his gaze dropped below her waist. The shaved pubis gave a prominence to her labia that was quite startling.

Tanya stared back at Grant's semi-nude body with frank approval while they discussed the choice of oils, then she lay face down on the couch. Julia watched him pour oil into his palms from the 'Tropical Essence' bottle. The musky, exotic mix was one of the sexiest of the oils. Tanya sighed deeply as he began to rub her feet, wriggling her crotch against the padded surface of the couch. As he worked his way up her thighs Julia could see that she was clenching and unclenching her buttocks in a rhythmic way that suggested she was practising internal pelvic exercises. When Grant began massaging her behind, letting his fingers slip tantalisingly between the two undulating cheeks, Tanya appeared to be riven by a series of wild convulsions.

'She couldn't have!' Julia whispered, in fascination. 'Not already, surely?'

It certainly looked like it. After the orgasmic twitching of her pelvis had quietened, Tanya lay inert until it was time for her to turn over. She settled on to her back with a languid, sensual ease then Grant began massaging her forehead. While he did so, Tanya's hands crept unashamedly to her breasts and soon she was alternately squeezing them and tweaking her erect pink nipples. Evidently she wasn't the sort to lie passively and let a man do all the work for her. Whether from impatience or a desire to gain the maximum erotic pleasure from the session, Tanya seemed determined to cram as many orgasms as possible into her hour with Grant.

The second time she came it was obvious. Julia could see her gasping, a deep rosy flush suffusing her chest, and her pelvis making violent thrusts into the air. Grant again looked surprised, but quickly adapted to what she wanted by curtailing the preliminaries and going straight for the groin. While Tanya continued to knead and pinch her swollen breasts, Grant plunged his finger inside her naked, open vagina and soon had her writhing and bucking ecstatically again.

Watching, Julia was overcome by a sick jealousy. The wonderful climax she'd received at Grant's hands now seemed tame beside the spectacle of this multi-orgasmic woman. Grant was grinning as he brought her to orgasm for a third time, as if it were all a huge joke. Tanya appeared to be in a state of perpetual climax, with every small movement of Grant's fingers in the wet pool of her sex triggering further waves of delight. Julia watched, heart racing, as he bent his lips to the hotly pulsating labia and tongued the thrusting nub of her clitoris. She was so frustrated that she couldn't bear to watch any more. Angrily she threw the switch and, tormented with insatiable desire, went through into her private sauna.

In a spirit of self-loathing she threw off her clothes and, sweating with the heat, she none-to-gently plunged her biggest vibrator in and out of her until she swiftly reached a shuddering climax. She did it again, and again, trying to prove that she could be multi-orgasmic too, but knowing that she was cheating. It was one thing to orgasm over and over with a dildo but quite another to experience the same thing with a man. God, how she hated Tanya Wentworth!

After Julia had showered and dressed she became ashamed of her earlier feelings. It was crazy to be jealous of Tanya. The woman had been blessed with a highly-sexed body and an uninhibited personality, that was all. There was no reason to believe that Grant felt any differently about her than about his other clients. She was easier to satisfy because she was not content to take a passive role but preferred to masturbate while she was being massaged. Julia could have done the same, if she'd been so inclined.

But that would have taken all the magic out of it, she reasoned. Her experience had been so special just because she'd had no hand in her own climax but, for the first time, had allowed a man to do it all for her. The wonder of it, and the deep sense of satisfaction, was still with her.

Feeling better about herself, Julia pondered once more the idea of Tanya being Jeremy's mistress. Had she persuaded him that he was some kind of superstud, that he alone had been able to produce multiple orgasms in her? Julia giggled at the very idea. From the way Tanya had behaved that morning it seemed that she was so highly charged she could come almost at will, regardless of who was making love to her. Now Julia had proof of it on video. She guessed that if ever Jeremy Cadstock needed his inflated ego puncturing that film would do it at a stroke.

By mid-afternoon Julia felt her energy level flagging. She needed a break, so she went down to the Healthfood Bar for a cup of Earl Grey and one of their delicious oat and apricot crunchies. As she sat at a corner table, pretending to read the *Gazette* but in reality eavesdropping on the conversation around her, she was suddenly aware of the eyes of several women swivelling towards the entrance.

Grant had come in, looking vibrantly healthy in a green T-shirt and black shorts. He saw her and waved. Then, when he'd collected his drink, he came over to her table.

'Mind if I join you?'

'Not at all,' Julia smiled, in her best business voice. 'I wanted to thank you for that message you left on my answerphone.'

'I meant it.' His eyes looked straight into hers, devastatingly blue, utterly sincere. Julia remembered what she had witnessed just a couple of hours before and felt a flush rise in her cheeks. She wanted to crawl under the table.

'I'm . . . er . . . glad you're settling in so well,' she went on, recovering a little.

'Today's been a good day so far,' he smiled, sipping his juice. 'I really seem to be getting into my stride.'

You can say that again! Julia thought.

'Do you have many appointments in the book for the rest of the week?'

'Well, Miss Wentworth has booked me again for Friday . . .'

You bet!

'. . . and I have Mrs Cadstock down for that day too.'

'Ah, Doreen!' Julia laid the *Gazette* down casually on the table between them so that the front page headline was clearly visible. 'I saw her right honourable husband on TV this morning, as a matter of fact. It seems he's appointed himself Guardian of Public Morals, or some such nonsense.'

Julia was watching Grant closely, but he gave nothing away. Although a lazy smile played at the corners of his mobile mouth he remained silent. Julia didn't push it. Instead she talked about the interview with *Healthy Life*. Grant seemed enthusiastic at the thought of the club getting some publicity.

'Mind you, I'm not sure we could take on many more members,' she laughed.

'So why not open another club?'

His question, uttered with all the naive simplicity of an outsider, stunned Julia. Up to now she'd thought only in terms of expanding within the premises. But if they really were reaching capacity and there was more demand, what Grant said made sense. If she didn't get in quick, there was no doubt that someone else would.

All thoughts of the threat from Jeremy Cadstock faded as Julia considered the idea in more depth. Of course it would mean that she would end up with less control, but the pay-off was the greater fulfilment of her dream, her dream of providing women with a safe, hygienic environment to explore their sensual and sexual potential.

'You've got a great thing going here, Julia,' Grant continued. 'It deserves to spread, possibly to another town. Maybe some kind of franchising mightn't be a bad idea . . .'

'Now hold on!' Julia laughed. But she felt warm

and excited inside. It was a bit like the old days, when she and Leo had planned the health club together, thinking big and seeing their dreams take off and become reality. In her lonely supremacy, Julia had forgotten how good it was to share some of those dreams.

He just smiled up at her, his face expressing simple pleasure, hiding nothing. As she left the Healthfood Bar Julia felt dirty. She'd been spying on him, secretly lusting after him, and she hated herself for it. Hated pretending everything was normal, that they were just employer and employee, while all the time every orifice of her body ached for him to fill it with his tongue, his fingers, his wonderful rampant prick. Yes, that most of all. If he could tease the most exquisite sensations out of her with his tongue, what wilder shores would that sturdy organ of his lead her to explore? The longing spread through her like devouring flames, making it hard for her to act as if nothing had happened. Steve called from the desk with a message and she answered him as if in a trance before returning to the sanctuary of her office.

Julia made her calls then sat day-dreaming, her mind buzzing with possibilities. The idea of a second club was slowly taking shape. She would build on her experience with *Sybarites*, make the new place bigger and better. She'd want to include a room for exercise classes – aerobics, yoga, maybe dance – and perhaps some women's health classes too. Why not make it a holistic health club with herbalists, acupuncturists and other complimentary practitioners in attendance? After all, she was already offering aromatherapy and spa treatments. Despite her own less than satisfactory experience, Julia had always believed that a woman's sexuality should be considered in the context of her whole well-being. If she found large enough premises she would be able to put her philosophy into practice.

'Bless you, Grant!' Julia said aloud, forgetting how she had cursed him earlier for his disastrous effect upon her equilibrium. She was itching to discuss further with him, to bounce ideas off him and see what they both could come up with. There was an instinctive understanding between them: if only she could forget his devastating attractiveness for five minutes and talk business.

She picked up the phone and got through to reception. Steve's voice answered her as if it were an outside call.

'Hullo, *Sybarites*. Can I help you?'

'Is Grant there?' she began, assuming he would recognise her voice.

But he appeared not to know her. Maybe I'm sounding more breathless than usual Julia thought, aware of how excited she was feeling. She was about to reveal her identity when Steve said, 'Did you want to book him for a massage?'

Julia hesitated. Of course she did want to, very much. With sudden recklessness she answered, 'Yes, please.'

'How about tomorrow, are you free in the morning? He has a slot at eleven.'

Julia knew she could still back out. But some crazy spirit of bravado had taken over and she said, 'That'll do fine, thanks.'

'Name?'

'Oh, yes. It's Jane. Jane . . .' she looked down at her desk for inspiration, and saw the local paper. 'Gazette.'

'*Gazette*? Could you spell that for me, please?'

'Yes. It's a . . . a French name. My mother . . . father was French.'

She spelt it out feeling an utter fool, sure that by

now Steve would have recognised her voice and presumed it was some kind of practical joke.

But he didn't. 'Thank you, Miss Gazette. I presume you are a member?'

'Yes, er . . . a new member. Miss Marquis only just interviewed me.'

'Oh, that explains why you aren't on the list yet then. Well, you're booked in with Grant for eleven o'clock.'

'Thank you. Goodbye.'

When she put down the phone Julia was trembling, half with fright and half with laughter. She'd actually booked herself a massage with Grant under a pseudonym! There was no way she could disguise herself and prolong the charade, however. If she did go through with it and keep her appointment she would have to stop this ridiculous game.

Still, she had wanted to see him and now she had an hour of his company all to herself. When she turned up she could explain that she wanted to talk through her business scheme in private, to make sure no one overheard them, and that had seemed the best way to do it. They would brainstorm for an hour then she would leave and that would be that. Mission accomplished. No sensual massage, no unseemly goings-on between employer and employee, no gossip, no hint of favouritism, no unprofessionalism . . .

'Oh God, who am I trying to kid?' Julia moaned aloud, her head in her hands.

Chapter Seven

FEELING NERVOUS AS a schoolgirl summoned to
the Head's office, Julia knocked at the door of the
massage room. She had by-passed the front desk,
for obvious reasons. Grant's deep, confident voice
invited her to enter and, with a tight feeling in her
throat and chest, she slipped in.

'Julia!' he exclaimed, his lips instantly curving into
a smile. 'I was expecting my next client, a Miss
Gazette. But if you . . .'

Julia cleared her throat and took a breath, trying
not to let her eyes drop below Grant's face where his
body was half exposed beneath the towelling robe.
'Actually, Grant, "Miss Gazette" doesn't exist. It's a
fake name. I used it to book an appointment with
you, so we could talk about that idea you gave me
yesterday.'

'You want to *talk*?'

'Er . . . yes. I thought we could be private here,
and . . .'

He came three steps towards her, a look of
sceptical amusement on his face. 'Just a minute, let's
get this straight. If you wanted to discuss something
with me why not call me to your office?'

'I . . . I just thought we could be . . . that this

85

might be more . . . intimate.'

Everything was breaking down: her ridiculous story, her nerve, her feigned impartiality, her whole credibility as his boss. He had only to stand there, exuding virility from every pore, and there was only one reality for her, the naked reality of her desire for him.

'There's nothing more intimate than a massage, is there? Are you sure that wasn't what you wanted, Julia? Are you sure you just want to talk?'

Mesmerised by his voice, she shook her head. He smiled gently, taking her hand, and she let him lead her towards a chair as if she were a child. When they were both seated he said, 'I've watched you over the week or so I've been here and it's fairly obvious to me that you're under a lot of stress. Of course, it's none of my business, but I think you really do need to relax. Why don't you let me give you a straight massage, right now. Not like last time, I mean a therapeutic treatment with marjoram and lavender, to calm you down. They're both good for stress and hypertension.'

His words struck a chord. How could she provide a service for other over-stressed women and not take advantage of it herself? She had allowed her professional scruples to deprive her of what she really needed.

Julia nodded. 'Perhaps you're right. I do tend to drive myself rather hard.'

'Okay. Let's get started then, shall we?'

When she emerged from the cubicle Julia deliberately averted her eyes from where Grant was oiling his hands, and went to lie, face down, on the couch. The minute she felt his warm, confident touch on her flesh Julia knew that this was just what she had been missing. Not the over-stimulation of sex but the deep relief of a complete letting-go. She sighed, delivering her body completely into Grant's keeping, like a baby with a trusted mother. Slowly the tensions that lurked beneath the surface of her skin began to melt away, leaving her feeling wonderfully slack and at peace with herself and the world.

The low, slow strokes over her back soon had her lulled into a doze. Julia was dimly aware of his firmer treatment of her buttocks, then the sweeping strokes again, down the backs of her thighs and calves. She was submerged in warm darkness, cocooned in a safe place where all the busy thoughts and tiresome feelings couldn't reach her. The strong, herby scent of the oil was working on her central nervous system, quietening her brain. By the time Grant reached her feet she was far away, floating in that subliminal state between sleep and waking.

He had to ask her twice to turn over. When she did, his hands were gentle upon her forehead. Delicate fingers described small circles around the sockets of her eyes, felt for her cheekbones, stroked along her jaw. Then they smoothed a path down her neck to her collar bone. Julia still felt beautifully sleepy and relaxed. Grant's flat palms were massaging just at the top of her chest with firm strokes and then he began to move lower, with light feathering movements of his fingertips. Julia felt a faint stirring in her breasts, like a slow wakening, but told herself to ignore it and remain relaxed. He had reached the subtle margin between the relatively neutral zone of her upper chest and the more sensitive breast tissue. She could feel exactly where the effect of his touch was more stimulating to her nerve-endings, more sensual, bordering on the sexual. Unable to help herself, Julia knew that her body was becoming eroticised, her nipples slowly ripening to hardness, her breasts swelling with yearning to be touched more firmly, more comprehensively.

I mustn't, she thought. I mustn't let myself get turned on.

But it was as futile as trying to stop her blood flowing or her heart beating. She could feel everything speeding up inside her, preparing her for love-making. There would be none, she was sure of that, but her fear was that Grant would know how urgently her body was wanting him. Could he feel the fierce throbbing of her various pulses as her blood cascaded through her veins? Could he see the tell-tale flush on her skin? Would the perfumed oil be sufficient to hide her increased sweat? Already she knew that her secret cleft was moistening, her private places opening and softening to admit a welcome invasion from outside. She couldn't help it. She just couldn't help herself.

It was natural, after all, Julia reminded herself as his palms avoided the tumid mounds of her breasts and began circling her navel. Natural to feel aroused by the touch of such an attractive man. For too long she had denied her sexuality, put all her energy into her business, tried to pretend that she didn't need a man. If you dammed up such powerful energy, sooner or later it would burst out, and that was what had happened when Grant gave her that first massage. What she was feeling now was an echo of that breaching of her defences, that was all. It was controllable, perfectly controllable, so long as she didn't panic, didn't over-react.

The heel of Grant's hand was pressing against her mons while he made firm circular motions on her abdomen. The consequent slight tugging of her pubic hairs was pulling up the hood of her clitoris, freeing it from its niche. Julie could feel the little nub hardening just below, becoming acutely sensitive. Deep within, her womb responded with an answering tremor. Soon the entire landscape of her body, from the crested mounds of her breasts to the warm cave of her vagina, was alive with tremulous illicit desire.

Julia told herself she could handle it. Once the massage was over she would retire to her room and give her frustrated body what it so obviously wanted. She only had to hold out for a few more minutes, until Grant had finished. Then she could go back to pretending to be cool, calm and efficient. He would never notice anything untoward, never know how much, and how shamefully, she had lusted after him. She had over-estimated her self-control, but once she got through this she would never allow herself to get into such a potentially dangerous situation again. And she would get through it. She must.

Just then Grant's hands slipped between her thighs and Julia made her fatal mistake.

She opened her eyes.

Grant was looking directly at her face, smiling slightly, his aquamarine eyes emitting a warm radiance. Julie felt her desire spiral out of control. She held out her arms to him.

'Come here!' she whispered throatily.

He moved in slowly until Julia could touch his broad, smooth back, feel the muscles working beneath the skin. His left hand clasped her breast and the confidence with which he rolled his thumb over her nipple told her he knew exactly what she wanted. Yet she didn't want it to be like last time, so restricted and one-sided. This time she wanted him to be involved. Julia looked up at his mouth and longed, achingly, to kiss him. One hand crept up to behind his strong neck, where her fingers tangled with his damp, silky hair, and soon his head was bending towards hers.

Grant's lips were full and soft, just brushing against her mouth at first, making shivers run all down her spine from her neck to her pelvis. Then she felt his tongue running along the more sensitive inner edge of her lips and the tingling contact intensified, this time passing right down through her body to her feet like a shock being earthed. He squeezed her breast gently, his fingers delicate on her skin, then traced a tickling, spiral path around its rosy cap with his nail, making both nipples tingle excitedly. She opened her mouth further and he pushed in deeper with his tongue, meeting hers halfway. Once she could taste the fresh sweetness of his saliva their kissing became deeper, more urgent. Julia groaned as she felt a shuddering response in her lower region, willing his hands to move down and ease the painful longing of her loins.

At last he swept down with his hand and crossed the tense hollow of her stomach to cup her mound. Julia tilted her hips, thrusting her pubes into his palm, then gave a great sigh of relief as his fingers finally parted the pouting outer lips, sought the softer tissues within and stroked them gently until they were bathed with warm liquid. Her clitoris, freed from its enveloping hood, longed to be rubbed and pleasured but his fingertips were searching out the entrance to her vagina, just below. Softly one small intruder found its way, began to wiggle about in the opening, making little sucking noises. Julia tried to force the pace by thrusting against him, but he held back and the intensity of her desire for him increased relentlessly until she grew desperate.

Grant sensed that she was needing more, but instead of stimulating her clitoris he moved his mouth down to her right breast and began to suckle hungrily. His hand moved from her sex to stroke her mons, stimulating her indirectly. Julia moaned, wondering how much longer this slow torment would continue. She knew what he was doing. He was relentlessly building up her desire for him, preventing her from coming too soon and spending the energy before it was at its peak. Well, now she wanted to know just how near to peaking he was himself. She needed direct evidence of his desire for her. Tentatively her hand reached out towards his G-string.

It was Grant's turn to groan as Julia felt the turgid length of him within the soft silken pouch. For a few seconds he backed away from her and she felt a swooping disappointment, but then she saw him quickly pull the skimpy garment over his tool and down his legs until he stood free of it. Julia took a few moments to survey the glory of his male nudity, the thick stalk rising from his dark curly hair like some exotic flower, blooming purple at the tip. It shuddered a little under the impact of her gaze, taut and ready for action. Julia felt an irresistible urge to move towards it. She grasped him by the buttocks and pulled him closer, then bent her head to his tool. It smelled strongly of musk. Tentatively she put out her tongue to lick his bulbous glans.

It was so long since she'd tasted the salt-lick of a man's penis. Now her tongue remembered, not just through its taste buds but also through the familiarity of the contours: deep-grooved helmet, jutting ridge, long smooth shank with its ribbing of veins. She explored it all, from tip to root.

Grant was breathing heavily now, in danger of losing control. He pulled her hands away and lifted up her head, kissing her quickly and roughly. Then he repositioned her on the couch and came up to kneel on all fours over her, so they could be in the 'sixty-nine' position. Julia cupped the heavy, dangling balls and wriggled down until she could take his prick between her lips. She felt his tongue bathe her feverish grooves with cool juice and sighed appreciatively. With the meaty length of him halfway in her mouth she gave herself up to his probing tongue that had already found her entrance and was seeing how far inside her it could reach.

Julia began to feel as if they were one animal, the serpent biting its own tail. Her whole body was on fire, and she could feel warm currents pulsing through Grant's tumid dick as her lips and tongue played around its top and sides. Never before had she been so completely physically attuned to a man, and she knew that she had begun the unstoppable rise towards orgasm once again. Her clitoris was like his penis, stiff and pulsating, and deep inside her vagina little ripples of pleasure were forming, infant waves of delight that would eventually reach a mighty crescendo of ecstasy.

Grant was thrusting gently in and out of her mouth now, and the suggestive movement was making her want him even more. She could imagine his gorgeously smooth and thick member probing where his tongue now was and the thought intensified her excitement. He seemed to sense that she wanted the pace to quicken and began to lick her clitoris in the light, rapid way he had before. She wriggled her hips in rhythmic lunges, round and round, up and down, however the sensation was keenest.

Now that Julia knew their mutual goal was near she was beyond wanting to prolong the build-up and she guessed he felt the same. A spirit of total abandonment had seized them both, bordering on frenzy, as they licked and sucked each other nearer and nearer to the edge. They hovered there for a few seconds, while Grant paused for breath. He continued with his fingers in her molten pussy, while she transferred her attention to his balls. Then he bent his head again for what Julia knew was the final stage of their joint ascent to the heights of passion.

Just as she knew she was about to reach her second blissful orgasm with him, a new, more tangy taste in her mouth told Julia that Grant was about to spill his seed and she pulled away, not wanting to swallow his sperm. Instead she cradled his cock in the chasm between her breasts and he groaned, thrusting his hand hard against her at the same time as he made his final thrust into her cleavage. She squirmed wildly against his wrist, letting her primed clitoris get the stimulation it needed to propel her into a climax. Instantly Grant came in a great gush that cascaded down her body. Their bellies slithered together while Julia continued to be riven by fiercely ecstatic convulsions, all emotions except grateful wonder blotted out, her body just one hotly focused centre of mindless sensation.

'Oh God!' she heard herself say as the inevitable slow fade began.

She was dimly aware of Grant lifting himself off her and lying beside her, squashed up against her yielding flesh as he cradled her in his arms. Slowly the realisation of what had just happened began to filter back through the spaced-out afterglow. Unable to help herself, Julia felt dread and shame flush through her. All the lovely feelings were spoilt as she contemplated the full significance of her seduction of Grant, one of her employees. She froze in his arms, horrified, wondering how she was going to face the consequences. What on earth must he think of her?

Slowly Julia tried to wriggle free from him, as if in doing so she could extricate herself from this embarrassing situation. She felt him stir, saw him open his eyes and stare up at her. It was like gazing into a misty blue sky. A rush of tenderness overtook her, making her want to cradle Grant's head in her arms and cover his face with kisses, but she snapped out of it and began to walk towards the shower. While she was washing him off her belly she might be able to think up some kind of explanation for her extraordinary loss of control.

But his voice stopped her in her tracks.

'Dear God!' he moaned. 'I've really screwed up, haven't I?'

Julia turned, bemused. Grant was sitting on the couch with his legs dangling over and his head in his hands. Slowly he turned to face her, his expression hang-dog. 'That was a test, wasn't it? You made a pass at me just to see if I could resist it, and I fell straight into it. Now you'll be thinking you can't trust me with clients.'

'No, Grant, I . . . ' Julia's first instinct was to deny it, but he hardly heard her.

'I wouldn't be like that again!' he insisted, his tone pleading. 'It was just with you. I . . . well, I do find you very attractive, but . . . God, this is making it worse! I'm sorry, Julia. I suppose you'll want to get rid of me now, and I wouldn't blame you. I know you have to be so careful here . . . '

Knowing she needed time to think, Julia said brusquely, 'I have to take a shower, Grant. We'll talk about this afterwards.'

He was still looking at her disconsolately when she left the room. Turning on the shower, Julia let the warm stream flow over her while she assessed the situation. It seemed that, miraculously, she'd been offered a reprieve from her own shame. If

Grant really thought she'd just been putting him to the test then he could still respect her, still believe she'd acted out of calculation, not out of sheer naked lust.

Yet she felt mean letting him persist in his delusion. He was obviously wrecked by the thought that he'd proved unprofessional and feared he would lose his job. Firing him had been the last thing on Julia's mind but perhaps that was the only course left to her now. If any testing had been done during the past hour it was of herself, not Grant. She'd been testing the strength of her self-control but her feelings for him had proved far too strong. Even now, the thought of his sturdy tool being at her command made her weak-kneed. What she'd just had from him had been wonderful but it had only made her want him more, and she knew she would go on wanting him. For both their sakes perhaps she should let him go.

Julia emerged from the shower draped in a towel and feeling desperately confused. Grant avoided her eye when she entered the cubicle to get dressed, and went straight into the shower after her. Carefully Julia resurrected her image of the efficient businesswoman, arranging her dark blonde hair into a loose French plait and spraying on some citrus-based cologne. By the time she was ready Grant was back in the massage room wearing his boxer shorts, a rope of towel around his neck. There was something boyishly appealing about the way he looked, with his hair in dark, spiky points from the shower. He was nervous and stammered a little when he tried to say what was obviously a prepared speech.

'L . . . look, I made a stupid m . . . mistake when I suggested you needed a massage,' he began. 'You came here wanting to talk and I should have let you do just that. The whole thing got out of hand, and I'm really sorry. I've enjoyed working here enormously, but . . .'

Grant's words reminded Julia of the idea he'd put into her mind, an idea which had promptly been driven out again once she'd lain down on the couch and put herself in his hands. Now, though, she was suddenly seeing everything from a different perspective.

'Grant, will you come up to my office when you're ready?' she asked coolly. 'I think we still need to talk.'

'Yes, of course.'

She turned away, but not before an image of his superb body had burned itself into her mind's eye. At the height of her rapture she'd wanted to know it completely, to have his flesh moulded to hers, contour for contour, and locked into the same rhythmic, ecstatic pulse.

Once in her office, Julia turned her plan over and over in her mind, examining it from all angles. What if, instead of sacking Grant, she offered him promotion, set him up as manager of her second health club? Then he would be her equal, free to be her lover if he so desired, without fear or favour. The idea excited her greatly but it was early days yet. Before she put it to Grant she would have to talk to her bank manager, her accountant.

While she waited for him to appear, Julia glanced wryly at the door of her viewing room. She hadn't set the video to record their encounter since she'd honestly believed that all they were going to do was chat. Some chance! Now she knew for sure that she and Grant were dynamite together, that they couldn't resist each other. By now he must know it too.

Grant's tentative knock at her door made her

smile again. He was expecting to be fired, not promoted. Her voice was friendly as she called 'Come in!' then pulled out a chair for him. He looked dejected, his normally level shoulders rounded in a slouch as he sat down, head bowed. With his knees apart he fiddled anxiously with his fingers while he waited for his boss to deliver the coup de grâce.

'I'm not entirely blaming you, Grant, for what happened this morning. It was as much a test of my own self-control as yours, and I wasn't exactly . . . restrained either.' He glanced up, surprise and faint hope in his blue eyes.

Seeing her smiling at him he risked a brief grin, then shrugged. 'I suppose we both got a bit carried away.'

'So I don't intend to dismiss you,' she went on. 'Provided you promise not to breathe a word about it to anyone, of course.'

Grant's whole posture changed and his face glowed. Julia wanted to hug him. She looked down at some papers on her desk instead, trying to compose herself.

'Of course I wouldn't! I won't let you down, Julia, I promise. I've never . . . ' he hesitated, perhaps remembering his session with the two model girls. 'Never become involved with any of my clients before, and I never will again. It's just that you . . .'

His words petered out, but she knew what he both longed and feared to say to her. She felt she knew him inside out, and one day they would be open books to each other. Just for now, though, she must be more circumspect.

'I'd still like to have that chat with you sometime soon,' she went on, briskly. 'About setting up a second club. I need to think about it a bit more first, though. Perhaps take some advice. Needless to say, that is also highly confidential.'

'You can trust me,' he said, simply.

'I do hope so.'

Julia was unable to prevent a note of uncertainty creeping into her voice. It worried her. *Did* she trust him, completely? Or was she in danger of letting her heart run away with her head? That was one of many things she must consider over the next few days.

'All right, Grant; you may go now. And remember what I've said, won't you?'

He nodded, rising. His bearing was proud now, strong and determined. Julia felt a pang of residual desire for him strike her loins, and a feeling in her stomach of being on the very top of a helter skelter and about to career headlong downwards. They shook hands firmly, which grounded her a little, then he left her alone.

'Grant, baby!' she sighed in an ironic American accent, sinking back into her chair as soon as the door had closed. 'You and I could make such sweet music together!'

At that moment she heard him whistling away down the corridor.

Chapter Eight

FOR THE REST of the week, Julia kept a close watch on Grant. He had appointments with Lou and Rebecca – separately, she was pleased to note – and with Jeremy Cadstock's two women. Grant's session with Doreen followed the same pattern as before: a straight massage, followed by at least five minutes of chat. Tanya's massage was as wildly orgasmic as her previous one, but this time Julia didn't feel the same aching envy. The way Tanya supplemented the masseur's expert caresses with her own masturbatory efforts now seemed self-centred, even rather sordid.

Remembering how she and Grant had found mutual satisfaction, Julia was filled with hope that they could soon become real lovers at last. Her financial advisors liked the idea of a second club and if, when they'd done their sums, it was still thought to be viable she would present Grant with her proposition. What she would do if he refused her didn't enter her head.

On her way home one evening Julia slipped into a quiet wine bar for a light supper. She was halfway through her glass of low-alcohol wine and cheese platter when a booming male voice greeted her.

'Julia! What a nice surprise!' She turned to see Leo smiling at her. He was with two other men but he quickly detached himself from them and came over to her corner. 'By yourself, my dear? May I join you?'

He had already pulled up a chair, plonked his bottle and glass of burgundy down on her table. Julia tried to look pleased to see him. At least if I put up with him now I won't have to see him again for another few months, she thought.

'How are you, Leo? You're looking well.'

'Not so bad. It's a pity there isn't a men's health club offering the same services as yours, or I'd be in far better shape.'

'Come come, you know men can get anything they want in this town.'

'Ah, but not in such tasteful surroundings as *Sybarites*. Maybe I should open a place myself, eh? Not quite the time though, I think.'

'Oh? Why not?'

'You know – what we were talking about on the phone the other day. A certain person who shall be nameless, since walls have ears, threatening to stir up a bit of mud.' His voice lowered. 'If I were you, Julia, I'd be thinking about your future very carefully. Not that I'm advocating actually throwing in the towel – no pun intended! – but a spot of house cleaning wouldn't do any harm while the heat's on. Tell your chaps to simulate, rather than stimulate, or something. And maybe they should wear something more clinical, like overalls.'

Julia felt a dozen petty annoyances surface. He really knew how to press her buttons, didn't he? Just the way he looked at her, with those knowing hazel eyes, as if he really knew best and she was just playing at being a businesswoman, made her cringe.

Added to which, at some level she was still half

seduced by his powerful masculine presence. He was like the big cat of his namesake, letting his prey go for now, giving it the illusion of freedom, just so that he could pounce on it again later. Was he waiting for her to fail so that he could come back and say, 'I told you so, but don't worry. I'll look after you now'?

Julia felt the urge to retaliate. 'I've no intention of changing anything, Leo. And certainly not because of some imagined threat from a publicity-seeking back-bencher.'

Leo's bushy brows knitted together, a warning sign she recognised of old. 'Don't dismiss him so lightly, Julia, or you'll regret it. He's canvassing opinion at the moment and getting a lot of support.'

'We'll see. But my members would be most disappointed if I changed my house rules. They like things just the way they are.'

'I'm sure they wouldn't like it if you ended up having to close down.'

'I've no intention of closing down. Quite the reverse, in fact. I'm thinking of expanding again soon.'

The words were out before she could stop herself. Not for the first time Leo had riled her into revealing more than she'd intended. She saw the flicker of interest in his eyes, the eager twitching of his mouth as if he were hungry for information, and softly cursed her impetuous tongue.

'Expanding? But I thought you'd already expanded as far as you could on that site with the new wing . . .'

Julia had to think quickly to prevent him from jumping to the obvious conclusion.

'Oh, I didn't mean expanding *literally*!' she told him airily. 'I was thinking in terms of the facilities we offer. I thought of maybe selling a few books and videos, exercise clothes, that sort of thing.'

101

'I see.' Leo had lost interest. 'Well, it's your business, Julia, and you must run it the way you think fit. But I'd think badly of myself if I didn't pass on what I hear on the grapevine from time to time.'

Julia felt herself softening towards him. 'Thanks, Leo. I do appreciate it.'

He gave one of the sweetly nostalgic smiles that even now had some residual power over her. 'I still care about you, Jules, always will, you know. Strange how neither of us has found anyone else, isn't it?'

He drained his glass and poured himself another. Julia recognised the alcohol-induced mood he was drifting into and wanted to leave.

'Speak for yourself,' she told him tartly, gathering up her bag and jacket from the empty seat beside her.

Leo's large head jerked up at her, his eyes struggling to comprehend. 'What's that? Are you saying you've got a thing going with someone? Something serious?'

Realising she'd made another mistake, Julia back-tracked quickly. 'Not really, no. I just didn't like you making assumptions, that's all.'

'What assumptions?'

'Never mind, forget it. Look, I really must go . . .'

Leo staggered to his feet too, knocking back the last of his wine. 'Would you do me an awfully big favour, sweetie? Would you give me a lift home? Only I came with those chaps but I don't want to drink any more. If I stay here and wait till they're ready for the off I'll end up rat-arsed, and I've got an important meeting tomorrow.'

All her instincts warned her not to. She could tell him to get a taxi. But he still had the power to make her feel guilty if she denied him and, affter all, it wouldn't be much out of her way. Besides, she reasoned further, she might learn something more to her advantage in the privacy of her car. Leo had a notoriously loose tongue when he'd been drinking.

So Julia waited patiently while he explained to his friends that his ex-wife was driving him home, endured their amused looks following his insinuation that they might end up in the sack together, and led the way out to the car park.

'This is awfully good of you, Jules,' he gushed as she opened the passenger door for him.

Once they were on their way Leo soon launched into a character assassination of Jeremy Cadstock.

'He has a mistress, you know,' he began. 'Quite a smasher. Saw her at Henley with him, last summer. Don't know what his wife thinks about it, if she knows. Damn fool, I say. Can't be a high profile killjoy if you're getting your jollies on the wrong side of the sheets, now can you?'

'I suppose he thinks he can get away with it. Even cabinet ministers have had their bit on the side in the past. As long as they're discreet . . .'

'Oh, he's discreet all right. Never seen in public with her in his home town. Mostly they go off on dirty weekends abroad, so my pal Josh tells me. He saw them at Bristol airport in the spring, on their way to Palma.'

'Still, someone unscrupulous could use it against him, I suppose.'

'Maybe. Maybe not. It would be a gamble. I mean, who really cares, these days?'

'But he seems bent on taking the high moral ground. Surely he can't preach one thing and practise another?'

Leo sighed. 'He's boxing clever. Says he's not against what people do in private, only what he calls public vice. Protecting minors, and all that. Maybe he's right, I don't know. But I should still watch

103

your step, Julia.'

'Ah well, you know what they say: "Never trouble trouble, till trouble troubles you".'

She was uncomfortably aware of the nearness of him as he sat slumped in his seat, reeking of alcohol. How many times had she driven him home like this, she thought ruefully.

In those days as soon as they were through the door of their detached, four-bedroomed house he would make a grab for her and force his furred tongue down her throat, grab her breasts or hitch up her skirt and try to reach through the leg of her panties (he'd never let her wear tights, only stockings). In the beginning Julia had found it all exciting, regarded his gropings as proof of his overwhelming desire for her. As a teenager, with low self-esteem as a result of an over-critical mother, she'd never believed any man would really want her. So when Leo came along, so charming and sophisticated, so thoughtful and tender (when he wasn't drunk), she had immediately believed herself to be in love with him.

Unwelcome images threatened to follow, so Julia quickly asked Leo about his own business interests, to take her mind off the past.

'Everything's going well, thanks. The shops are struggling a bit, of course, but then we are supposed to be in a recession. You wouldn't think it the way the casino's going, though!'

Leo had a third share in a chain of betting shops and a casino. Julia showed polite interest, but was secretly glad that she had nothing more to do with all that. She felt the trade was dirty, encouraging people's addiction to Lady Luck, robbing their families of hard-earned wages. In her view it was entirely hypocritical of people to tolerate his type of business and condemn hers.

104

'Actually, I'm thinking of buying some property just round the corner from you,' he went on. Julia's interest sharpened. 'Millers, the jewellers. Went bankrupt, remember? It's a nice big site. Workshops out the back. I could do a lot with that.'

'Really? What would you turn it into?'

'Amusements, probably. This town could do with another arcade now the one down Market Street has packed up.'

Julia smiled to herself. Suppose she outbid him for the site and built her second club there? That would be quite a coup. Leo would be bound to take her more seriously as a businesswoman if she managed to spoil his plans. He'd always had a grudging respect for rivals.

They reached the block of luxury flats where Leo now lived and Julia drew up outside.

'It's been really nice seeing you this evening, sweetheart,' he cooed, fumbling with his seatbelt. He leaned across to take her in his arms, but she automatically flinched back.

'Come on, just a kiss for old time's sake!' he wheedled.

'All right, then. Just one.'

She gave him a peck on the cheek, but he pulled her close and managed to thrust his tongue into her mouth, filling her nostrils with yeasty fumes. Julia nearly gagged. She pushed against his chest but he was cushioned by flab and her hands made little impact.

'God, Julia, I still want you!' he groaned. 'You're as gorgeous as ever. Why did we ever split?'

She managed to get her face free of him, at least. Taking the tone she knew was least likely to rouse his inflammable temper, she said in a motherly voice, 'Now don't be naughty, Leo. You said you've got an important meeting tomorrow, remember? It's time you went home.'

'Home?' He turned his dismal, bloodshot eyes skyward. 'What's a home without a woman in it? Just a hole, that's all. A hole to crawl into.'

Julia got out of her seat and went round to the other side to help him out. She was relieved when he stood up of his own accord and began to lurch down the drive.

'Goodnight, Leo!' she called after him.

He waved and staggered on. For a moment Julia felt pity for him, but then she remembered how he had crushed her, humiliated her – sometimes in public – and made her feel just as worthless as her mother had. The old anger re-surfaced. She got back into her car and drove away fast.

Julia's encounter with Leo made her all the more determined to get it together with Grant as soon as possible. Her experience of the two men couldn't have been more different. Leo had imposed himself upon her, regardless of her own needs, and tried to turn her into his mindless plaything. Grant, on the other hand, seemed to respect her as a person, and he certainly knew how to satisfy her physically. They communicated well too. Julia's gut instinct told her that their relationship could really take off – *if* they could free themselves from their present unequal positions.

Next day, Julia visited the auctioneers dealing with the Millers site. She viewed the property and found it ideal for her purposes, then went to see her bank manager who, much to her relief, gave her the go-ahead. Now, all that remained was for her to share the news with Grant and put her proposition to him.

Back at the club in the late afternoon, Julia went to look at the appointments to see when Grant might be free. He'd already gone home and tomorrow was his day off, so she would have to wait until Friday. She happened to glance down the other bookings and was amazed to see Tanya Wentworth's name with 'Private Sauna' beside it.

Steven noticed her surprise and said, *sotto voce*, 'Interesting eh, Miss Julia?'

She frowned, not wanting to encourage idle speculation amongst her employees. 'It's not for us to pry, Steven. Discretion at all times, remember?' Even so she couldn't resist giving him a playful wink before she went.

It was extraordinary, though. The sauna could be booked for private sessions for an extra fee, and the women members were allowed to bring in their male partners for that facility only. It was always an evening session, and Tanya had booked it for eight o'clock that night. Julia knew that Steven had been thinking the same as she: would she have the nerve to bring Jeremy Cadstock in, to make love with him in the sauna?

Then a more sinister interpretation struck her. What if she'd invited the MP to come and snoop around? Ben Soames would be on duty that evening. She must warn him to keep a close eye on the couple, not let them roam round the place at will. They must be directed straight to the sauna and then straight out again.

Julia couldn't remember whether she'd had a camera installed in the sauna. If she had, she'd never bothered to view that particular room. Quickly she accessed the camera installation plan that she still kept on her computer files. Yes, there it was. A frisson of excitement went through her as Julia realised that not only could she witness what went on between Tanya and her 'guest' but she could film it as well!

Even so it seemed incredible that Jeremy would

compromise his reputation right at the start of his much-publicised campaign. As eight o'clock neared Julia installed herself in front of the screen, feeling the tension mount inside her. All she'd had since breakfast were two coffees, two cups of herbal tea and a fruit juice. The hollow fluttering in her stomach could have been hunger pains as much as apprehension: they felt much the same.

Promptly at eight, the door to the sauna opened and a naked Tanya entered, followed by . . . Doreen! Julia's first reaction was shock. Surely they weren't going to make it a threesome? But when Tanya shut the door behind them and Doreen poured water on the brazier Julia felt a mixture of disappointment and relief strike her. It was just two old friends having a relaxing sauna and a gossip, that was all. What a shame she hadn't had a mike installed, though. She would dearly love to know what those two women found to talk about when they were completely alone.

Julia watched as Tanya poured some oil into her palm and handed the phial to Doreen, who did likewise. But then, instead of anointing their own bodies, the two women began to oil each other. From the slow and loving way their hands moved over each other's curves, it began to dawn on Julia that they were more than just good friends. She gasped at the realisation that Tanya and Doreen were lovers, and probably had been for many years. Since their schooldays, even.

Her mind racing with speculation, Julia found her suspicions were confirmed when the two women embraced closely and then kissed. Tanya was fondling Doreen's large breasts, her own firmer specimens jutting with sexual tension as her tongue flicked in and out of her friend's mouth. Soon their hands were roving everywhere as their passion flourished in the warm atmosphere, and the slippery gleam of their bodies gave them the air of two wet fish floundering on dry land.

It wasn't long before Tanya had her head between Doreen's thighs and was giving her a thorough licking. She seemed to be the more active of the pair, and Julia suspected that she was highly over-sexed. She was rubbing her own clitoris as she performed cunnilingus on Doreen, and as her friend reached her first climax she was obviously in the throes of orgasm herself.

They lay together for a while after that, kissing and caressing, whispering together. Julia found her attention wandering as thoughts of intrigue crowded in on her. If Tanya really was Jeremy's mistress, did Doreen know about it? Did Jeremy know about his wife's bi-sexuality?

The potential for scandal seemed huge, especially since Julia now had it all on video. Surely the politician wouldn't dare make any moves towards closing down *Sybarites* if he knew that both his wife and his mistress were members. But what if he didn't know anything? What if, busy at Westminster, he knew nothing about what his wife and her best friend, who was also his mistress, got up to behind his back?

Her mind moved on as it so often did to Grant. He'd seemed to be very pally with Doreen – was he perhaps her confidant in all this? Then she recalled Tanya's words about the cruise her friend had been on. Was it possible that Tanya had been on that cruise too? The possibility that the three of them might have cooked up some sinister plot involving the politician was almost too scary to contemplate.

On screen the two women were slowly resuming their erotic play, mouths sucking eagerly at protruding nipples, but Julia had seen enough. She stripped off and went into her own private sauna, not because she was aroused but because she wanted to relax, and think. However she soon found herself on the verge of dozing off. I've been working too hard lately, she told herself. She began to fantasise about going away with Grant to some tropical beach and desirous urges crept up on her. But when she grew aware of the itch between her legs Julia rose and took a shower. She was tired of self-pleasuring, living only for the next time she could be with Grant. Hopefully that next time would be soon, and they would feel free to become the lovers they already, secretly, were.

After checking that the video had recorded the lesbian scene in the sauna, Julia left her office. It was half-past nine and as she crossed the reception area the doors to the health suite swung open and Tanya and Doreen appeared, laughing. They saw Julia and grew more reserved. On impulse, she decided to talk to them. Approaching with a fixed smile she said, 'Hullo, ladies. Relaxing after a hard day? I hope you're enjoying our club, Mrs Cadstock. Has Tanya been showing you the ropes?'

She was proud of herself for being able to keep a straight face. Tanya, however, couldn't suppress a grin and turned away to hide it. Doreen just looked flustered.

'Oh . . . yes, Miss Marquis.'

' "Julia", please . . .'

'I . . . um . . . think you've done very well here. Most . . . er . . . relaxing.'

'I noticed that you've both availed yourself of the services of our newest masseur, Grant,' she smiled. 'Did you know him from before too, Tanya?'

'Oh no!' she said, quickly. 'He was Doreen's find.'

'Well, I'm always interested in taking on high quality staff. If either of you know of people you could recommend, in any capacity, I'd be glad to interview them.'

Moving off through the door, Julia congratulated herself on her cool handling of the situation. She would be needing new staff soon, for the second club, and she already owed Doreen a debt of gratitude for introducing her to Grant. It was often better to go by personal recommendation than rely on public advertising.

The unsolved mystery of the Cadstock love triangle continued to plague Julia as she drove home. Not that she was normally given to speculation about other people's sex lives, but given the circumstances she felt she had every right to take an interest. The question that worried her above all was how much did Grant know? Was he somehow involved in their tangled web? Perhaps it was just as well that she was planning to elevate him from the position of masseur to manager of her new club. That way she would have some kind of hold over him . . .

Julia stopped short, hating herself for being so calculating about the man she believed she was falling in love with. Yes, love. It was not a word she'd ever thought she would use about herself. In the early days of her marriage she had told Leo she loved him because that was what he'd wanted to hear, but she'd had no idea of the real meaning of the word. The depths of feeling that she had now been plunged into by Grant represented new and uncharted waters, and she was more than a little scared. Was it possible to be afraid of getting what you wanted most in the world? Because that was how she felt.

She got home to find another message from him on her answerphone.

'Julia, I'm sorry to bother you at home but I can

hardly sleep for thinking about what happened the other day. I'm very grateful to you for giving me a second chance, but I still feel bad about it. I've never ... well, it's never happened before. I've always managed to stay detached from my clients and ... Oh hell! I don't really know what I'm trying to say. Except that you did mention wanting to talk to me about the idea of opening another club. I'm free on Friday evening, if you want to see me then. So ... well, goodbye Julia. And ... thanks a lot.'

She played it three times over, just to hear the sound of his voice again. The undertone of confusion that ran through his message made Julia suspect that he might be in the same state as her: unable to sleep, unable to forget their last steamy session, unable to think of much else. The attraction between them was obvious, undeniable. And Julia was going to do her best to get rid of the main obstacle to their love. But what were the other possible impediments: a steady girlfriend, perhaps? A 'burnt-fingers' mentality that prevented him from forming strong attachments? Ghosts from the past?

Well, she would find out on Friday night whether there was any hope for them or not.

Chapter Nine

GRANT WAS COMING to dinner, straight after work. Julia had left the club early on Friday to prepare for the momentous event, but now panic had set in. The food was all ready to be cooked in her kitchen, she had showered and washed her hair. But now, as she stood in front of her open wardrobe contemplating what to wear, she began to wonder what she would do if Grant turned down her proposal.

Apart from the personal humiliation involved, her career seemed partly dependent on him. The idea of opening a second club was a good one, but would she have the heart to go ahead with it if Grant were not involved? Worse, could she bear to go on employing him as a masseur, to be tormented daily by the knowledge that he was caressing some other woman while she sat in her office tortured by desire for him?

Sighing, Julia reached for a shimmery blue dress then changed her mind and went for black velour leggings and an outsize pink T-shirt. She didn't want to appear overdressed. Suddenly she changed her mind about the food, too. She had planned to impress him with a home-made béarnaise sauce for the steak, but she decided to offer a choice of mustard instead. What was she trying to do, she asked herself – find a way to his heart through his stomach? He either wanted her or he didn't, and no amount of window dressing could alter that.

By the time the doorbell rang, at twenty past eight, Julia had worked herself up into quite a state. She knew she looked good, with her fine blonde hair brushed into a smooth bob and her make-up understated. She smelled good too, exuding a subtle mist of *Samsara*. But inside she was a mess, the emotional equivalent of a frowzy slut, and her heart was leaden as she opened the door.

'Hullo, Julia. Hope I'm not too early.'

She was totally unprepared for the flowers. An extravagant bouquet of roses and exotic lilies was thrust into her arms with a slightly sheepish grin, and her mood lightened instantly.

'How lovely! But you shouldn't have, Grant. This was only meant to be a business dinner.' ('Liar!' she told herself, wryly.)

He gave her one of his irresistibly boyish grins. It was the smile of a much-loved son who knows he can get away with almost anything. 'I realise that, but I wanted to thank you for being so forgiving. I know I've made some mistakes, but I really will be more careful in future.'

She hung Grant's jacket on a peg in the hall, put his briefcase near the door then led the way into her stylishly furnished sitting room.

'I know you will,' she told him, over her shoulder. 'I've every confidence in you, Grant, as I hope to prove this evening.'

The beautiful flowers deserved her most precious container. Julia took an exquisite green and pink Gallé vase – a present to herself when *Sybarites* had opened – filled it with water and set the pre-arranged bouquet in it. While they sipped white wine and nibbled Japanese rice crackers, Grant congratulated her on her taste.

'This décor is so well thought-out,' he commented, looking around him. 'Did you plan it all yourself?'

'Yes. It's been such fun having a place all my own. When I was first married, my ex-husband called in a design consultant for our house and I was completely excluded from the whole process. I ended up feeling as if I lived in a hotel rather than my own home.'

Grant frowned. 'How dreadful!'

'Well, I've made up for it since. Not just here, but at the club too. I enjoyed designing the pool area and massage suite enormously, and the members seem to like it. When Leo owned the place I was little more than a glorified receptionist.'

'It sounds like divorce has been good for you,' Grant smiled. But then his face clouded. 'I wish I could say the same.'

'You're divorced too?' Julia's buoyant mood flattened a little.

'Yes, usual story. Married too young. No kids, though, thank goodness. I went away on the boats to get it all out of my system.'

'And did it work?'

He shrugged 'Time will tell. I won't believe I'm really over it until I've become totally involved with someone else.'

Grant gave her a level look that sent her pulse soaring. Was he sending her a coded message? It certainly felt like it.

Not wanting to raise her hopes too soon, Julia excused herself and went to put the finishing touches to the meal. Soon they were seated at her table, with Grant tucking eagerly into her food. Julia wished she had more of an appetite. There was a knot of nervous energy in her stomach that just wouldn't shift, and it was all she could do to push the mouthfuls down.

She couldn't help watching him as he ate, though. Her eyes first lingered on the mobile mouth that had so satisfyingly melded with the most intimate parts of her body, then on those capable hands whose caresses still lingered, like tactile echoes, on her skin.

'That was delicious!' he smiled after the cheese, finishing the wine in his glass.

'Coffee and brandy?'

They moved to the sofa and their mood mellowed, aided by some soft background jazz. Julia knew it was now or never, and her hand shook slightly as she poured the coffee. It didn't help to have him sitting less than an arm's length away.

'You said you had something to discuss with me,' Grant prompted her, evidently curious. 'Is it about the idea of opening a new club?'

'Yes. I've been doing my homework, making a few enquiries, and it seems the scheme could get off the ground.'

'Julia! That's marvellous!' His enthusiasm sounded genuine.

'I've got financial backing. I've even found a possible site, not far from *Sybarites*. But I need a good manager to run it, and that's where you come in.'

'*Me?*' Grant was looking at her incredulously.

'Well, it was partly your idea.'

'But I've no experience of that kind. None at all.'

Julia smiled. 'Neither had I when I took over *Sybarites*. I never went to business college, all I had was a bit of office experience when Leo let me work at the reception desk. But I learned on the job. I watched closely everything that Leo and the rest of his staff did, learned from their example – and from their mistakes! It's surprising how much you can pick up as you go along. And I'll always be there to advise you, of course.'

Grant stared thoughtfully into his brandy glass. 'I'm very flattered that you've asked me, Julia, of course I am. But why me? There must be a hundred managers out there with good track records. Why pick an untried guy like me?'

Julia couldn't tell him the truth. Couldn't tell him that it was the only way she could think of to get him on a more equal footing with her, so she wouldn't feel so bad about wanting him.

'I can't explain, except to say I have a gut feeling you could do it. You'd be working closely under my supervision at first, of course, but you'd have to be a hundred per cent committed to the job. Think it over. You don't have to give me your answer right away, but I'd like to know by the end of next week.'

Grant's face became unreadable. Julia turned away in confusion, unsure of herself, and topped up their coffees. She was so afraid he was going to turn her down flat.

But when she dared to look back at him, he was smiling.

'Julia, I don't know quite how to say this, but you've read my mind. Years ago, when I was first married. I had the idea of opening a health club and running it with Allie, my wife. I soon realised she wasn't up to it, of course. More to the point she wasn't interested, although she pretended to be. So that idea went into limbo, along with my dreams of a perfect marriage and two-point-four kids. Now I'm thinking maybe it's an idea whose time has come.'

Julia laughed, suddenly feeling that everything

was falling into place, for both of them. 'A dream come true, maybe?'

His face brightened, and his eyes suddenly shone like blue steel. 'Hell, Julia, why not? I don't need time to think about it. I used to think of little else. If I don't take the chance now, it may never come again. I'll do it!'

She clasped his hand in both of hers. It felt strong and true, a hand to be trusted. Filled with a deep certainty that everything was going to be all right, she gave him an open, tender smile. 'I'm so glad, Grant.'

His answering smile was a touch rueful. 'I may be making a big mistake. We both might.'

'That's what I thought when I changed the health club into *Sybarites*. My ex-husband wasn't exactly encouraging. But you've got to follow your instincts, Grant. And mine are telling me that you're the man I should appoint as manager.'

'I'll give it my best shot, Julia. I promise.'

'Let's drink to that.' They raised their brandy glasses. 'To the new *Sybarites*, or whatever we decide to call it.'

They looked at each other, eyes glowing, and after they had drunk the toast and put their glasses back on to the coffee table Julia sensed an air of unfinished business between them. I'm not imagining it, she thought as, still locked in each others' gaze, their heads slowly converged. Grant put up his hand to stroke her hair where it hung loose about her shoulder, and she heard his breath being exhaled in a sigh. She knew he was remembering, the same as she was, and her whole body began to thrill with vibrant life. His face moved closer, so close that she could smell the faint of trace of *Fahrenheit* cologne, but then she heard him murmur, 'Madness! This is madness!'

He stopped leaning towards her, looked about to turn away, but she put a hand up to his cheek. It felt smooth but slightly clammy, as if he were perspiring just a little.

Grant's seductive eyes teased her mercilessly as he repeated what he'd said earlier. 'I may be making a big mistake. We both might.'

'We both made a mistake the first time, didn't we? This time around it will be different. No man ever made me feel like you did, Grant. Like you said before, if I don't take the chance now it may never come again.'

Within seconds his lips were hard on hers, testing the firmness of her intent, searching for an answer to his unspoken questions. Never before had she felt so exposed, as if she were being strip-searched by a kiss. He wanted to know if she meant what she'd said before. Not just with her mouth but with her eyes, when they'd looked at him, and with her body, when she'd climaxed for him. He wanted to know what was in her heart and he wouldn't rest until he'd found out. His kiss was an inquisition, and her respose was a joyful surrendering to the truth.

Julia knew she must have given him the answer he'd been longing for because soon his desire for her was evident, the hard shape of him pushing against her thigh. His hands went beneath her loose top to find the taut cones of her bra and the treasures within. Impatiently he plundered the lacy material, pulling the cups down roughly until he could feel her bare flesh, already ripe and filled out with arousal. With equal impatience Julia reluctantly broke from his kiss to pull the T-shirt over her head and unhitch her bra, letting her breasts spring free.

'Oh Julia, you've got one hell of a body!' Grant groaned.

She was still fumbling with her clothes, rolling

down her leggings, struggling to free herself from the only barrier that now remained between her and total abandonment to Grant's lips and hands. Soon Julia lay almost naked on the sofa, except for a pair of black lace panties. She could see the tanned skin and dark hairs at the open neck of Grant's white shirt and she wanted the licence she'd given him, the freedom to touch and hold warm, willing flesh.

Grant sensed her need before she spoke of it. Quickly he undid his buttons, first at the cuffs then down the front of his shirt, laying bare his beautifully sculptured chest. Julia laid her hands flat against it, felt the slight tickle of the hairs, the smooth warmth beneath. She nestled close, smelling the raw male odour that emitted from his armpits, along with the fainter scent of his cologne and the darker, muskier undertone that spelt out, more clearly than words, his desire for her.

She began to embrace him but then, finding the sofa too cramped, Julia whispered, 'Let's go into the bedroom.'

For a second he looked down at her, his eyes bleary with controlled passion. A silent message flashed out to her, 'Are you quite sure?' Julia understood perfectly, smiled and gave firm nod. Then he lifted her bodily off the sofa and carried her through the door. She clung to him, loving the novel sensation of being hi-jacked out of her role as efficient businesswoman and turned into someone soft and compliant, someone who relished being swept off her feet and tenderly manhandled. When Leo had behaved like this, she reflected briefly, it had been to subjugate and humiliate her. With Grant, however, it felt entirely different. He was about to bring out the best in her, not quash it.

Entering her own bedroom Julia found it now looked quite different. She had never made love in this room and now she knew why: she had been saving herself for this man, awaiting this perfect occasion to turn her beloved sanctuary into the equivalent of a honeymoon suite. Gently Grant deposited her on the white lace bedspread and stood looking down at her, his hands in the belt of his jeans, while she wriggled impatiently out of her panties. He might have been a victorious hunter, looked down on his captured prey, yet Julia felt no fear. Only a deeply grateful surrendering to the inevitable.

'You're beautiful,' he murmured.

She smiled up at him, seeing him framed by the ornate gilt mirror that hung against the cream textured silk wallpaper. Now he looked every inch the Hollywood sex god, she thought with amusement, as his hands moved to his fly. Slowly he unzipped himself, watching her all the time, delighting in her tremulous anticipation. Down came the Levi's, to be casually side-stepped, then his hands went to the waistband of his navy silk boxer shorts. First they had to be eased carefully over his very obvious erection. Julia found she was holding her breath as the shiny purple tip of his glans became visible, followed by the ribbed splendour of his fully extended shaft. The slip of material slithered down his lean thighs to fall in a pool on the floor, but Julia only had eyes for his penis. She had been too close to it before, had seen it for only a few seconds before her hungry lips had tasted its savoury length. Now, in the context of his finely moulded torso and sturdy legs, she could appreciate its true proportion. Tall and thick it reared to his navel unabashed, an instrument built for pleasure and proud of its calling. Julia, always a lover of beautiful things, began to understand why the *lingam* was worshipped by eastern cults, deemed an object of veneration by men and women alike. The understanding hit her with the force of a mystical initiation.

Grant held his prick in his left hand and, with a questioning look, used his right hand to mime putting on a condom. Julia produced a packet from the bedside cupboard and threw it to him, watching while he quickly slipped a second skin over his swollen glans and rolled it down the shaft.

In a dream she watched him move towards her as she lay sprawled, wide-legged, on the bed. She knew she was already wet and completely open to him, despite the fact that there had been hardly any foreplay. Now he was kneeling before her, lowering his head to nuzzle at the source of her sex. Julia moaned aloud as the fresh softness of his tongue met her sensitive inner lips and stroked them apart, insinuating itself just inside her opening. Her desire for him was intense, knowing that this time there were no holds barred and soon she would be filled with the full length of him, plundering all the secrets of her hidden cave and revealing treasures she hadn't even known she possessed.

Grant raised his head and positioned himself on his knees, his face glowing with dark joy. Julia felt her womb convulse at the thought of him entering her, sending strong shudders all through her pelvic region. Then he put the tip of his glans between her labia and rubbed softly against her. Again he threw her a tender, questioning look and she smiled back at him, pleased that they were able to communicate so effectively without words and grateful to him for giving her, even now, a chance to have second thoughts.

Except that she had none. Her thoughts were all of Grant, and how much she loved and wanted him. There was no room in her head for other considerations, not while her body was so loudly proclaiming her desire. Gradually she felt the bulbous head of his organ nudge into her, plugging her up, and she wanted to thrust down vigorously, to feel the whole length of him inside her. But Grant kept her at bay, staying just inside her where her tight lower mouth was kissing him beautifully, opening and closing on his glans in unconscious rhythm. He leaned forward and put both hands on her breasts, grasping them firmly, and Julia felt new sensations sweep through her, throwing her into a state of even more voluptuous abandonment and linking her tingling nipples with what was happening down below.

Julia could feel her clitoris harden, grow sensitive, as the delicate tissues around it were stretched and stimulated. The throbbing intensifed as he head of Grant's tool ventured a little further inside her, so that she could feel the ridge behind his glans rubbing back and forth against her vaginal entrance. Using the muscles there she caressed him, milked him, made him give a little guttural cry of surprised pleasure, but still he remained in control, only half of him inside her, making sure she was good and ready for when he finally decided to take the plunge.

In the end it was Julia who couldn't bear the suspense. She wanted him to fill her completely, thrust in up to the hilt, and so she pushed her hips forward and took the full length of him into her warm, receptive wetness. At once the walls of her vagina tightened around him, feeling the solid flesh fit perfectly within her own soft cushioning, and she heard him moan with renewed pleasure. Beneath her hands his buttocks were working rhythmically, plunging his penis in and out of her so that she felt herself moving like a dancer in sweet concord with him, weaving and circling her hips to gain the maximum stimulation for her jutting clitoris.

Grant bent his head to take her left nipple in his mouth, holding her breast as if it were a delicious cake and he were nibbling at the cherry on top. The feelings that spread through her from his gently suckling lips took her to new heights of sensual abandon. Within seconds she was coming, her neck arched back as the plunging motions of Grant's member sent ripples of pure ecstasy throughout her body. Her head was spinning, her toes tingling, and all regions in between were thrilling to her multiple climaxes, all thoughts lost in wave after wave of mindless orgasm.

Dimly, Julia was aware that Grant was holding back, making small thrusts only as her senses spun wildly from the pleasure of his prick. At last she collapsed back on to the bed, her capacity for pleasure momentarily exhausted, and felt Grant's tiny, butterfly kisses around her navel. She opened her eyes and saw him smiling up at her.

'Wonderful!' he breathed. 'You're truly wonderful, Julia.'

'No, it's you,' she insisted, softly. 'Your loving, that's what's wonderful.'

His shaft was still spearing into her, slightly quicker, stirring up faint echoes. Julia lay still and passive, letting him set the pace, not trying to reciprocate. Grant's eyes shot blue fire at her as he let his own desire have its head, and soon she was responding once more, this time wanting the climax to be mutual. Slowly she roused herself from her post-coital trance and began to embrace him with her inner walls, teasing her clitoris to prominence again, feeling him harden and push more urgently, engrossed in his own rise towards oblivion. His head nuzzled against her breasts, tickling her skin

124

with his silky hair and turning her nipples into hungry buds of longing.

'Julia!' he moaned, as he neared his finale.

She folded her legs around behind his back and arched up her pelvis so that he could plunder deeper, deep into her sexual heart. She wanted him to possess her more completely than any man had before. Already he had brought her more pleasure than she'd ever known, and now she wanted to do the same for him. Julia could feel herself opening up further to him, her very centre seemed to yield to his persistent rhythm, until she too was being swept away with him on the high tide of passion.

There was a brief moment of suspense when they seemed poised, at maximum tension, on the edge of their consummation. Then Grant made a series of rapid plunges and they both felt a shuddering release, still floating on the edge of each other's consciousness as they gave themselves up to their own pulsating raptures. Julia heard him groan loudly, three times, before collapsing on to her breast. Still in the glowing after-throes of her second orgasm, she turned sideways and clasped him to her so they could lie more comfortably. Then exhaustion intervened and, for around half an hour, they dozed in each other's arms.

Julia woke first. Seeing Grant lying beside her, his right arm flung up over his head and his left arm around her shoulder, she was filled with an overwhelming tenderness. Sleeping, he seemed so open and defenceless: the crescents of his lids with their dark fringes, the full lips relaxed and slightly open, the utter relaxation of his powerful muscles and, above all, the wilted softness of his dehydrated penis, gave him an air of vulnerability that moved her deeply.

His eyelids flickered open and, seeing her looking

at him, he gave a broad smile. They kissed, briefly but sweetly, and she snuggled in to his chest.

'Bit more comfortable than the massage couch, don't you think?' he said wickedly.

'Mm!' Julia's hand slipped down to cradle the soft slackness of his balls. 'Maybe you'll let me give *you* a massage sometime.'

'I'd like that.'

Somewhere outside a clock began to chime midnight. Julia froze, afraid that he would have to go, afraid there might be an abrupt end to this incredible prolongation of bliss.

He seemed to sense her thoughts.

'Mind if I stay the night, Julia? Somehow I don't feel in a fit state to drive home.'

'Of course you can!' she laughed with relief, cuddling him. 'In fact, I was planning to tie you to the bedpost, just to make sure.'

'You and whose army?'

They fell to teasing one another, giggling, play-fighting like kids, and Julia knew she had never been so happy, so carefree. Inevitably their antics evolved into erotic play, this time with Julia astride him, setting the pace. She rolled down the condom over his erect phallus then lowered herself on to it and leaned forward, making her heavy breasts swing within Grant's eager grasp as she rode his sturdy erection, teasing his balls with featherlight touches from behind. Up she rose until the taut ring of her pussy was over his glans, only just maintaining contact. For a while she would hover there, caressing his ultra-sensitive tip while he moaned his tormented delight, then she would suddenly force herself down on him, filling herself up with the rigid column of flesh and making him thrust urgently with his hips. She would let him have his head for a while, both of them pumping away with wild abandon, but then she would rise up and hold herself aloof again, biding her time.

'Tormentress!' he eventually accused her with a grin. 'That's enough of your tricks, vixen!'

Taking her by the hands he suddenly slid from beneath her and turned her around, lifting her hips so that he could penetrate her from behind. She gasped as he came hard into her, his pubic bone flush against the plump cushion of her behind. Now she was content to let him have his way, shafting her long and hard in a steady rhythm that soon had her on the verge of orgasm. His hands found her boobs, pressed flat against the bed, and he squeezed her nipples mercilessly as he gathered momentum for his climax. Julia squirmed with delight as she felt him shoot into her, sending answering ripples of sensation flooding through her innermost being and out to the very extremities of her body.

'Oh, that was so *good*!' she gasped as she flattened herself, exhausted, on the bed. She lay there while Grant caressed her buttocks and thighs with lazy, delicious strokes, prolonging her physical gratification beyond orgasm into a wonderfully sensual drowsiness. More satisfying even than that, however, was the sense of completeness she felt, the marvellous feeling that she had at last found the man who could help her be entirely herself.

Eventually they crept between the sheets, and Julia felt warm and secure in his embrace. Could loving possibly be this simple, she asked herself in the brief period before sleep overtook her. She knew that tomorrow, or the next day, there would be talk, and yet more talk, but for the time being she was content just to lie in his arms, dreaming. It had been absolutely perfect. If she never experienced another night as good as this she could at least claim that now she knew what making love was all about.

127

Chapter Ten

WAKING NEXT TO Grant was like coming out of a beautiful dream and finding herself in an even more beautiful one. Julia slipped carefully from the bed and went to make breakfast. By the time she brought in the tray he was awake, smiling seductively at her from between the crumpled white cotton sheets.

'I feel like I'm on my honeymon,' he said. 'Except that my honeymoon was nowhere near as good as this.'

'Neither was mine!'

Julia joined him in bed. Snuggling up while balancing the tray on her knees was tricky, but she did her best. She offered him orange juice with a smile. 'I'll tell you about mine if you'll tell me about yours!'

'There's not much to tell, really. Allie wanted us to go somewhere exotic, so I chose Bournemouth.' Julia giggled. 'We hadn't much money, needless to say, although her parents helped us out. They didn't approve of me, of course, but they tried not to show it.'

'Leo was an orphan so I was spared all that. The weird thing was, I had the feeling that *he* didn't approve of me marrying him. It was as if he thought I couldn't really be a worthwhile person if I hitched myself to him. But go on, Grant. I'm fascinated!'

'Well, the service and reception went off okay I suppose, but I was secretly dreading our wedding night. I was only nineteen.'

'Same age as me, when I got married.'

'Look, am I telling this story or are you?'

Julia looked mock-mortified. 'Sorry. But do have a croissant while they're still hot.'

'But I'll get crumbs in my navel!'

'Don't worry, I'll lick them out. So, as you were saying . . .'

'As I was saying, our wedding night wasn't quite what we'd expected. I wasn't very experienced, although I'd had two girlfriends before Allie. She'd wanted to wait until we were married before having sex, so although we'd heavy-petted a lot she was still a virgin. I think she was hoping for instant bliss, but it just didn't happen for her despite my best efforts.'

'Mm, I know the feeling.'

'Don't you mean the "not feeling"?'

'Silly! Oh damn!'

'What's the matter?'

'Crumbs in *my* belly button now. And strawberry jam.'

'Mm! Let me at it!'

There was a pause while Julia deposited the tray on the floor and Grant bent his head to her stomach. When he had thoroughly cleansed her navel, sending fluttering messages out to all parts of her body in the process, he proceeded upwards to lick her breasts and suck gently on her tumid nipples until she knew there could be no stopping what they'd started.

This time they took it slowly, savouring each

other to the full. Grant stretched out and let her massage his passive body. Through her hands she got to know every inch of him: the broad, flat slopes of his chest with the light smattering of hairs; the concave basin of his stomach, leading down to his strong thighs. There were little idiosyncrasies too: the way his pubic hair was coiled in little, springy curls; the small, crescent-shaped scar on his knee; the slight overlapping of two of his toes. Julia delighted in the way he felt. His flesh was firm and elastic under her fingers, but although his muscles were solid they were not the over pumped distortions of the body-builder. More like the anatomy of a working animal in good condition.

After a while Grant began to caress her back, then stroked her breasts while she knelt astride him. At first she thought they might be in for an action replay of last night, but soon he sat up and, after making sure she was ready for him, slipped on a condom and made her sit in his lap. Once he was safely docked inside her they embraced and began to rock gently back and forth, kissing gently and cradling each other tenderly. Julia felt the erotic fire re-kindle inside her, rising up from her loins to her breasts and back again, building an electrical circuit of ever-heightening desire.

'Rock-a-bye, baby,' he crooned softly, his hands travelling down her back to clench her buttocks as they swayed back and forth.

Julia felt safe and protected, secure inside the encircling pen of his arms. She had never been like this with Leo, always been on her guard at some level. And after her divorce she'd believed that she could never trust a man again. Now she marvelled that, within the space of a few short weeks, Grant had won her total confidence.

Inside her body she could feel him growing

harder, the firm root of his penis pressing against the folds of her labia. At the top of her engorged nether lips she could feel her own nub of pleasure rising to meet him, becoming roused by the indirect stimulation. The memory of her previous orgasms served to reinforce her desire, and she shuddered inwardly as she recognised the start of the long, exquisite ascent towards the peak of sensation.

It seemed Grant could feel it too, the sensitive response of her body that indicated her deep need for him. His lovely smile met her eyes, telling her that he knew, and his delight in her arousal quickened the process so that soon she was working her pelvis more urgently, sighing and moaning as her clitoris rubbed itself against his rock-hard shaft.

'Julia!' he whispered fervently in her ear, as if even hearing her name turned him on. 'Oh, Julia! You're . . . indescribable!'

'Is that indescribably bad, or indescribably good?' she teased him.

'Both! You're a tantalising mixture of both!'

Their brief interchange inspired rougher play, with the pair of them now making determined efforts to reach their climax. Julia pushed her breasts out towards him provocatively and he took a firm hold of them, working her stretched nipples with his thumbs to make them tingle intensely. In return, she reached behind her back to find his balls, and proceeded to scratch and tickle them while they rocked to and fro with mounting excitement.

Suddenly, with a burst of hot energy, Grant laid her down on her back and plunged into her from above. His deep penetration made her groan, and after just a few thrusts she could feel her climax approaching. This time it was fierce and prolonged, racking her through and through with strong convulsions that soon triggered Grant's orgasm too.

As the ripples died away inside her, leaving a glowing warmth, she could feel the spurting of his seed and the wild beating of his heart keeping time with her own.

While they lay quietly recovering in each other's arms, Julia thought, 'I love him'. It was still too new for her, unknown territory, but the certainty was there. She longed to tell him, but was wary of frightening him off, so she settled for saying, casually, 'Well if I'd felt like this the morning after *my* wedding night I doubt if I'd ever have got divorced!'

Grant chuckled, kissing her. 'You really think that's what marriage is all about?'

'It's got to be the foundation, surely. If that's not there, how can anything else work?'

'I'm sure you're right. Allie and I used to have so many petty arguments, like over whose turn it was to make the coffee. Talking of which . . .'

He got up and went into her kitchen. She loved hearing him clatter about, trying to figure out how her grinder and espresso machine worked. When he finally reappeared, bearing the tray with a triumphant grin, she realised how much joy she was getting from every trivial moment of their time together.

'I could live like this,' she thought happily.

At noon they decided, reluctantly, that it was time to get up. But that didn't mean giving up their sensual exploration of each other's bodies – at least, not immediately. The minute Julia turned on the shower he was in there with her, smoothing the Guerlain shower gel over her body until it lathered, then giving all her nooks and crannies a thorough cleansing. She did the same for him, but before long she wanted to taste the clean essence of him, and knelt to take his prick in her mouth. Once the scent of the gel had been licked from his shaft his own musky odour reached her nostrils and she sighed contentedly, feeling his penis grow ever longer and stronger under the ministrations of her tongue, tasting the droplets of salty liquor while she fondled his balls. Grant let her suck him to a climax, his juices spilling straight into her eager mouth. It was another first for her, and she loved it.

They soaped each other again, gently washing away the last traces of their love-play, then towelled each other dry.

'Happy?' he asked her, suddenly, when they were getting dressed in her bedroom.

She turned, smiling, in surprise. 'What do you think?'

'I think you look happier than I've ever seen any woman look. You know, Julia, the first time I saw you I wanted to make you smile. Oh, you were giving me a smile all right, but it was a routine, professional one, the sort you gave to anyone. I knew there was another kind of smile lurking in you somewhere, a big, open-hearted one, and I wanted to be the one to bring it out. Well, now I've succeeded, and it's made *me* very happy.'

Julia beamed even wider and his lips answered her. They kissed with passionate tenderness, then Grant said, 'Well, Ms Smiley, what are we going to do for the rest of the weekend?'

'The *weekend*?' She'd hardly dared hope for as much.

'Well, it's now Saturday lunch-time. I suppose I *could* go home right now and do my laundry and shopping, make a few calls, catch up on my bills . . .'

'Don't even think about it!' she laughed. 'If that's the best you can come up with in the way of plans for the weekend you might as well stay here.'

'My opinion entirely.' He glanced through the

133

window. 'I'm down to work tomorrow afternoon, but until then I'm at your disposal. How about a picnic? Looks like it'll be a nice afternoon.'

While they drove to a nearby lake and beauty spot, Grant continued the story of his marriage. From the way he spoke it was clear that he felt guilty about allowing himself to be tied down too young. Allie didn't seem a bad sort, the way he described her. Their marriage sounded as if it had been one of quiet misery and petty bickering rather than anything profoundly damaging.

When he asked her about her time with Leo, however, Julia found it hard to talk. Not that Grant wasn't a sympathetic listener, but she hesitated to burden him with the shadow that still came over her whenever she thought about her ex-husband. It was still a gloriously sunny afternoon and she didn't want to cloud it.

So Julia settled for a brief outline of their five years together. When she described some of the ways in which Leo had tried to suppress her personality, Grant said, 'But how could he pretend to love you, yet not want you to be yourself?'

'Good question. I really think he wanted a compliant doll, someone to screw in private and show off to his friends in public. He caught me young, you see, before I'd had enough time to develop a sense of what I wanted out of life. Or of who I was, even.'

'Well you've certainly progressed a long way since.'

'It was hard persuading Leo to let me work in his health club, even as a receptionist. We struck a bargain that if he let me work for three years I'd start a family at the end of it. Except I got the taste for business, and realised that I didn't want a family. Not with him, anyway. I felt really guilty when I realised that what I really wanted was a divorce. I knew that what he'd feared all along was coming true. He'd given me a taste of independence and now I wanted more. I felt terrible.'

'But if he hadn't squashed you in the first place . . .'

Julia sighed. 'Yes, yes, I know. But that's all water under the bridge. At least we're on relatively friendly terms now.'

'You still see him?'

'Occasionally. All his business is in this area so there's no question of him moving away. And I wanted the health club as my part of the divorce settlement, so there was no way I was going to give that up either. I'd fought hard enough for it.'

'Allie and I made a clean break,' Grant told her. 'She moved to Birmingham, to be near her folks, and now she's married with two kids.'

Julia gave him a sidelong look. 'No regrets?'

He turned, smiling, and shook his head. 'None whatever. I worked through most of my feelings on the boats. Nothing like a few years on the high seas to help you get things in perspective.'

They found a spot near the lake and took out the impromptu picnic they'd brought. Julia lay back on the plaid rug while Grant poured the chilled wine. She could see dark green branches of fir with blue sky in the gaps, and hear bird song. How long was it since she'd felt this relaxed and peaceful?

'Oh, this is wonderful!' she sighed.

Grant's face loomed above her. 'You're wonderful.'

'Okay, so I'm wonderful. But so are you. Let's eat.'

'Let's kiss first.'

His lips roused her dangerously, so that when his hand slipped under her T-shirt she wanted more.

135

But there were people boating on the lake and their shouts disturbed her.

'Hey, Grant, let's have some wine.'

When they had eaten and drunk their fill, Grant suggested a walk through the woods. They cleared the picnic away and replaced the residue in the car, but Grant folded the rug and slung it over his shoulder with a wink.

'Just in case we find a really secluded spot!'

Walking hand in hand with him Julia felt as if she were starting all over again. Not even the early days with Leo had approached this degree of carefree happiness. She remembered always feeling uptight, wondering how to behave and what he expected of her. This time she knew that there was no hidden agenda. She and Grant were being perfectly themselves, and if there were obstacles on the horizon – as, realistically, she knew there would be – then she was confident that they could overcome them together.

'I want to talk more to you about my plans for the new club,' she told him as they walked along an overgrown path, thick with pine needles. 'But that can wait. This weekend is just for us. If I could, I'd make it last forever.' She giggled. 'My God, I can't believe I just said that!'

Grant gave her a stern look. 'Julia! I'd never have believed you were a closet romantic!'

'Neither would I!'

They found a place, hidden amongst the pines and scrubby undergrowth, where they could spread their rug unseen. It was dappled with light and shade, a little chill out of the sun. Grant took her in his arms and began kissing her again, lifting up her top so that he could nuzzle into her cleavage. Julia put her hands behind her back and unhooked her bra, giving him access to her already swelling breasts.

Soon they were lying naked together on the rug, with Grant mouthing her nipples while his fingers slowly insinuated themselves between her moist labia.

'I've never made love in the open before,' she admitted in a whisper. 'It wasn't Leo's style.'

'Well it *is* mine. I'm a "Nature Boy" at heart!' he grinned down at her.

As if to prove his point he plucked a nearby fern and began teasing her breasts with it. The curled fronds were rough on her nipples, rousing them further. He swept his improvised fan down her body, brushing it over her sex and down her thighs with a featherlight touch. Julia moaned softly, wanting him inside her yet knowing that the longer he prolonged their foreplay the sweeter it would be.

She snatched a fern for herself and began to wave it at his genitals. A mock fight ensued, and Julia felt her heart pounding with excitement as he pinned her down by the thighs and began to lick at her already hard clitoris. Grant's hands swept upwards over her stomach, reached for the undersides of her breasts and finally grasped big handfuls of them, making her gasp with sudden longing. His tongue was about as far inside her as it could go by now, imitating the powerful thrusts of his penis. His hands left her body momentarily to enable them to find the condom in his jeans pocket and slip it on, but all the while he kept his busy tongue working on her, making her slick and ready for his entry.

It was with a cry of relief that Grant finally plunged into her, getting a steady rhythm going at once with his hands under her buttocks to protect her from the hard ground. Yet the very firmness of the earth beneath them was a new experience for Julia. She found she could thrust her hips back at him more effectively, synchronise with him more completely so that they were like horizontal dancers, perfectly attuned to each other.

Julia opened her eyes and saw the sky again, far above them, and the greenery all around. Making love in such a setting seemed so natural, so right, putting them on a level with all animal life. Even the little cries they made, the sighs and moans, sounded more animal than human. Giving herself up to the dark currents of energy that were swirling through her, Julia was in a mindless state of rapture, high on the crest of a wave that seemed to go on forever without breaking. There was no climax, no sudden consummation of their loving, only an endlessly sweet flow, each dependent on the other, complimenting the other, leading into a blurring of the boundaries between their bodies.

After what seemed both timeless and a very long time, Grant sank down wearily into her arms. Neither of them had come, but neither of them had needed to. Locked into a perfect, rocking rhythm they had reached the heights and stayed there, blended in bliss.

Looking into each other's eyes there seemed no need for words. They lay and dozed, listening to the intermittent bird song, until the sound of a dog barking not far off brought them back to humdrum reality.

'Better get dressed, I suppose,' Grant said, reluctantly.

By the time a man and his Labrador appeared through the trees the pair were decent again, if a little abashed. The stranger bade them a gruff 'Good afternoon' and strode on. Julia looked at Grant and giggled.

They got back to Julia's flat in the early evening, decided against going out for a meal and settled for what she could rustle up. Then they sat side by side on the sofa eating pizza and watching a silly horror movie. They were both exhausted, yet somehow found the energy to make love in the shower and proceed to the bedroom, where they almost fell asleep in the middle of their love-play. Snuggling up, Julia relished just being in his arms as she drifted off.

Sunday morning began lazily, with Grant fetching breakfast then promptly making her forget all about such mundane preoccupations as coffee and toast. This time he took her from behind, kneeling on all fours, his enthusiasm for her tight but ample buttocks knowing no bounds. Julia loved the way he reached beneath her to pull at her dangling nipples or feel the heavy weights of her breasts as they fell like ripe fruit into his palms. She loved, too, the way his balls slapped against her thighs as he pounded her, and the helping hand he gave her clitoris from time to time, propelling her rapidly towards a long and satisfying climax.

Looking into Grant's eyes afterwards, she knew it would soon be time for him to leave. He was on duty at the club that afternoon – all the masseurs had to do a Saturday or a Sunday unless they gave prior notice – and there was no way she would try to interfere with the rota. Julia knew she was already treading on tricky ground, and until Grant was safely installed as manager of the new club she must be careful not to show him any favouritism.

'I have to go, Julia,' he said when, shaved and dressed, he quickly downed his second cup of coffee. 'Will I see you tomorrow?'

'At work, yes. And maybe later – if you're free, that is?'

He smiled and drew near, smelling of the cologne she'd already come to associate with him. 'No, I'm not free . . .' He laughed at her disappointed face. 'I'm totally captivated – by you!'

They kissed joyfully until, hitching his jacket down from the peg in the hall, he moved to the door and was gone. Julia heard him whistling his way down the stairs then peeped through the curtain to watch him get into his car. Even at a distance he looked extremely dishy. When they were finally an established couple women would cast longing glances at him, envious ones at her. But she wouldn't be jealous because there would be no need. Julia was confident that the bond cemented between them that weekend would stick like Superglue.

For a while Julia floated about the flat unsure what to do with the rest of the day. She couldn't stop thinking about him, about his body, his smile, his presence that still seemed to linger everywhere. She decided to clear away the breakfast things and took the tray through to the kitchen but, entering the hall, she suddenly noticed Grant's briefcase. It was still standing in the corner by the front door, where she'd put it – had it really been only two nights ago?

Setting down the tray she went to pick it up, her mind pondering what to do. If he needed it that afternoon she could drive down to the club with it, but that might look a bit too much as if she were chasing him. Otherwise, she could take it in tomorrow. To help her make up her mind she opened the catch and looked inside.

There was a slim folder of plastic containing a few sheets of paper. Julia took it out. On the cover a label read: *Sybarites* – Report on Massage Service.

Intrigued, Julia opened the folder and began to read. Her eyes widened incredulously as she scanned down the page. It was soon clear that Grant had been making a detailed report of the way the club was run and of his own activities within the privacy of the massage room. Some of the detail was very graphic indeed. He also referred to remarks made, in confidence, by other masseurs, even by Julia herself. She stared, white-faced, at the neatly-typed pages. In the wrong hands this could be very damaging indeed, so why had he made this report?

Then, at the end of the folder, she found a slip of paper torn from a writing pad. On it was scrawled the brief message, 'Keep up the good work! D.'

'D' – for 'Doreen'? Cold fingers clutched at Julia's heart as she contemplated the possibility that Grant might have made his report for the wife of Jeremy Cadstock. She remembered how she'd seen them talking together, behaving like conspirators, and her dreadful fear intensified. Was it possible that the man she'd been making ecstatic love with for the past two days and nights was secretly planning to betray her?

Chapter Eleven

WORSE, EVEN, THAN the torment of suspecting Grant was the prospect of facing him. For several hours Julia paced around her flat trying to find some way of excusing him, but the evidence seemed too damning. She thought of going straight to the club that afternoon but kept putting it off until it was too late. Then she wondered about trying to reach him at home. She picked up the phone but replaced it without dialling. Tomorrow would be soon enough to shatter both their dreams, she finally decided. She needed time to get used to the idea that the man she'd thought of as her lover and partner was really her enemy.

Several times she read through the frank report, seeking other possible reasons for its existence, but the amount of explicit detail made it quite clear that it had been written to expose *Sybarites* as a den of iniquity. Her bewilderment soon turned to anger as she thought of the loving she and Grant had shared that weekend, how absolutely she had trusted him. How could he have made love to her over and over, with such passion and tenderness, knowing that he had the means to destroy her business? He'd even agreed to be manager of the new club. Had he intended to go on spying for the Cadstocks, to ruin her second business venture the same way that he planned to ruin the first?

Many times Julia rehearsed how she would approach him, what she would say to him, but there seemed no satisfactory way. She even considered giving his briefcase back to him without comment, as if she'd never opened it, never seen the shattering evidence inside. But the thought of carrying on as if nothing had happened was impossible. She would never be able to look him in the eye again, let alone make love with him. Never!

At the realisation that all her beautiful dreams had been stillborn, Julia burst into tears. This was worse, far worse, than her disillusionment with Leo. What she'd never had from her ex, she could never miss. With Grant she had found paradise and now, like Eve, she had been banished from that blissful Eden forever. It was all too cruel.

Somehow Julia managed to pull herself together next morning, after a tearful and sleepless night. She looked like she felt – terrible, but a shower and some disguising make-up helped her to put on a front. Dressed in a sober navy suit with a white blouse, her hair swept into a French plait, Julia drove to work more slowly than usual. It was the equivalent of dragging her feet, not wanting to face the inevitable, but once she'd found her place in the car park she knew there was no turning back.

At reception, Steven was his usual cheery self.

'Morning, Miss Julia. Had a nice weekend?'

The irony of it almost made her weep. Pulling herself together she said, 'Not bad. Any messages for me?'

'Only a call from the editor of that magazine – *Healthy Life*? She says the article will be printed in the October issue and she's sent a copy for your approval.'

If I still have a health club by then, Julia thought miserably. She forced a smile. 'Fine. Oh, and is Grant around yet?'

'I think he has a client. I'll just check . . . Yes, he's busy until eleven. His next appointment after that is not till two.'

'Will you tell him I'd like to see him in my office, then? As soon as he can make it after eleven.'

'Yes, Miss Julia.'

Unable to concentrate on office work, Julia went to work out in the gym for an hour. Maybe this will get rid of some of my anger, she thought as she cycled away furiously. At ten she went for a shower, but it only reminded her of making love with Grant and her tears began to flow as freely as the spraying water. Feeling horribly vulnerable inside she did her best to restore her cool and efficient image again, knowing that the meeting she would have in half an hour would be the most difficult, and probably the most traumatic, she'd ever had to face.

Grant appeared at five past eleven. He knocked, put his head round the door and grinned at her, his blue eyes so full of joyful tenderness that Julia almost burst into tears again. Somehow she managed to stay in control, asking him to sit down in a grave tone that soon wiped the smile off his face.

'Julia?' he questioned, uncertainly. 'Is everything all right?'

'I'm afraid not.' She lifted up the folder from her desk and saw him blanch at the sight of it. Some black-hearted part of her was pleased by his distress, wanted him to be as upset by his exposure as she'd been by his treachery.

He half rose from his chair, his handsome features twisted in distress. 'Oh God, it was in my briefcase. I must have left it at your place. Look, I can explain . . .'

'Can you, Grant?' Julia was surprised at how calm she sounded, how subtly threatening. 'This is all your own work, isn't it?'

'Yes, but . . . Julia, I know how bad it must look but please let me tell my side of the story. I can promise you that I never intended to hurt you, or your business.'

She raised her eyebrows sceptically. 'Okay, I'll listen. But this had better be good.'

He looked so despondent, slumped there before her, that she almost felt sorry for him. Only the slow fuse of her anger, burning away in her solar plexus, saved her from giving in to her weaker impulses – her longing to embrace him, tell him she forgave him and still, painful though it was, loved him.

'You know that I've known Doreen Cadstock for a while . . .' Julia's wrath flared up. So she'd guessed right! She nodded, grimly. 'Well, I was doing that report for her. She got me to promise to do it before I even got taken on here. In fact, she made it a condition of giving me a recommendation.'

'She wanted you to get a job here just so you could *spy* for her?'

'In a way, yes. But she's got nothing against you, or *Sybarites*. It's her husband and Tanya that she wants to hurt. It's all rather complicated, but she and Tanya are old friends . . .'

'A bit more than that, I'd say!'

'You know about them?'

Julia gave an impatient nod. 'Yes. Go on.'

'Well, Tanya is also Jeremy's mistress. And she doesn't know that Doreen knows.'

Julia snorted, her eyes swivelling to the ceiling. 'Tell me something *I* don't know.'

'Okay, Julia. Look, this is very difficult for me . . .'

'Hah!'

145

'And for you too, I know. But you must believe that I didn't intend to harm you. At first I didn't realise what I was getting into. Doreen wants to end Tanya's affair with Jeremy and keep her all to herself. She wanted a report from me so she could threaten to tell the press that her husband's mistress also had sex with her masseur.'

Julia's mouth twisted into a sneer. 'And you're saying that couldn't possibly harm *me*, right?'

He had the grace to squirm a little. 'All right, I know it sounds bad. But telling the press was only going to be a last resort. She wanted to scare her husband into giving Tanya up, threaten him with exposure, that's all. Then he started on this campaign of his and the situation became more complicated.'

'I'll say!'

'It was also more complicated for me, because by then I'd fallen for you, and I didn't want to do anything to jeopardise your business.'

'Decent of you! So how did you plan to wriggle out of that one?'

'I wasn't sure. I thought maybe I could string Doreen along a little, persuade her not to use such incriminating evidence. Tell her it was enough to threaten him without dragging the club into it. I hoped that would work.'

He threw her a look of such pitiful appeal that she almost relented. But there seemed to be too many loopholes in his story. She believed that he was in league with Doreen, now that she'd seen them together, but suppose the MP's wife had been spinning Grant a line? Suppose she'd been acting for her husband all along, collecting evidence that he could use in his campaign against *Sybarites*?

'How much does she know already?' Julia snapped. 'Has she read this report?'

'Only a bit of it. I had to show her, to prove I was keeping my side of the bargain. But that's the only copy, and she hasn't read it all.'

'You're sure she hasn't photocopied it?'

'Quite sure. She only glanced through it in my presence. I wouldn't let her take it away.'

'Well at least the damage has been limited up to now. But you realise this is a serious breach of our security agreement, don't you? I shall have to destroy this report, and I have no option but to dismiss you. Naturally the proposal I made to you about managing the new club is also null and void.'

'I know how you feel, Julia . . .'

'Do you? Do you really?'

He shrugged, miserably. 'Maybe not entirely. But I can't tell you how much I regret this. After the weekend I was hoping . . . well, I suppose that's history now. What an idiot I've been! I should never have agreed to that woman's conditions. I should have applied for the job on my own merit, it was just that she was a member and . . . oh God, Julia, please believe I never intended to hurt you!'

'What do they say about the Road to Hell, Grant? Well, I've been to hell and back for the past twenty-four hours. You've ruined my personal life, threatened my business. Oh God, Grant, if you only knew . . .'

Julia buried her face in her hands, not wanting him to see her face made ugly by her pain. Even now she half longed for him to put his arms around her and comfort her, tell her everything was going to be all right. But he kept his distance, sat in his chair mumbling about how sorry he was, and her heart hardened against him even more.

'Well, at least I didn't do what that woman really wanted, and make a video of me giving Tanya a massage.'

'What?'

'That's what she asked me to do, but I refused.'

Julia gave a bitter laugh. 'You didn't need to. I've already got videos of you with all your clients. No doubt you'd have wheedled that out of me sooner or later.'

When she looked up Grant was frowning fiercely, making Julia wish she hadn't said that. He rose and leaned over the desk, his face dark with suspicion.

'Are you saying you've been secretly filming me?'

'Not just you, Grant. Don't get paranoid. I have cameras in all the massage rooms. It's the only way I can keep a check on my masseurs, make sure they're not going too far with their clients.'

'So you've got film of me with Tanya, and Doreen, and . . . my God, even with *you*?'

'That's right.'

He stepped back from the desk, with a look of distaste. 'You mean you sit here, like some voyeuristic pervert, watching everything that goes on? This is unbelievable!'

Seeing Grant so obviously disturbed by the thought that he'd been spied on, Julia felt a perverse urge to hurt him further. It was becoming an absurd game of spy and counter-spy, but she would play it through to the finish. Julia rose and, taking the key from her handbag, unlocked the door of her viewing room. Grant entered in disbelief, but the sight of the large monitor with its buttons linked to the massage rooms made him gasp.

'Show me!' he barked grimly.

Unwilling to expose any of the other masseurs, Julia switched on the channel that was tuned to his own room. It was empty, of course, but he recognised it at once.

'Where's the film of our session?' he snapped, opening a drawer. 'I want to see it.'

'You can't. It's at home,' she told him, coolly.

'So you could sit playing with yourself while you watch it, I suppose!' he sneered. 'God, how pathetic! Show me the film of my session with Tanya, then!'

'No, I won't. It's none of your business.'

'I'll find the damn thing myself, then!'

He yanked open another drawer, found some videos inside and went through reading the labels then tossing them aside. Seeing the door to her sauna standing slightly ajar, he strode forward and, before she could stop him, had gone in there.

'Grant, that's private—'

Too late. He'd found her box of tricks and was holding up a large dildo with incredulous distaste. 'God, woman, you're sick!'

'It's none of your business, Grant! If you don't get out of here at once I'll ring Steven and get him to throw you out—'

He rounded on her suddenly and, for one horrible moment, she feared he was going to strike her. Then the flame of naked aggression in his eyes died down. He went back through to her office and sank into his chair again while Julia returned to her desk, struggling to retain some sense of normality.

'The way I run my club and what I do in private are entirely my concern,' she said, trying to sound reasonable. 'I trusted you, Grant, and you let me down. End of story.' She took a deep breath and raised her head, staring blankly at him while she intoned the ritual for dismissal.

'You will honour any appointments already made for this week,' she told him. 'But, if you remember, you're still on three months' probation and I can give you a week's notice.'

'Yes.' He looked downcast, began to rise awkwardly from his chair.

'Goodbye, Grant,' Julia said, briskly, pretending

to get back to her paperwork. He gave her a long, stony stare. 'I'm prepared to give you a standard reference after you leave here, but that's all.'

Grant left abruptly without saying another word. As soon as he'd gone Julia collapsed in a heap on her desk. Her previous anger with Grant was compounded by her humiliation. Whatever image he'd had of her during their weekend of sexual pleasure must now be tarnished by the knowledge that she got off on watching her masseurs at work, and used sex toys to gain her satisfaction. If only she'd been able to explain to him that they were no substitute for the real, loving experiences they'd shared.

Later that afternoon, when Julia had tried unsuccessfully to bury herself in work and finally decided to give up and go home, Steven hailed her from the front desk.

'Miss Julia, could I have a word?'

'Yes, Steven. What is it?'

'It's about Mr Delaney. He's told me not to book him any more clients after this week. I thought I'd better check with you . . .'

Julia tried to keep her tone impersonal. 'That's correct, Steven. As from the end of this week Mr Delaney will no longer be in my employ.'

'You're sacking him?' He sounded incredulous. 'But I thought he was doing so well!'

There was an odd look on Steven's face, as if he knew more than he was letting on. Julia wondered if she'd been the subject of gossip, if her staff had guessed what had been going on between their boss and the new masseur, and her heart sank.

'He was here on trial, and he decided the job wasn't what he wanted,' she lied smoothly. 'I shall have to re-advertise, unfortunately. I hope a replacement won't be too hard to find.'

'You had quite a job last time, didn't you? Shame Mr Delaney wasn't happy here, although he certainly seemed to be. He was popular with the members, too. Both of those model girls . . .'

'Thank you, Steve, that's enough!' Julia said sharply. 'I'm going home now. See you tomorrow.'

'Goodbye then, Miss Julia.'

Steven still looked faintly puzzled but Julia hoped she could trust him not to spread further rumours. More to the point, what about Grant: could she trust him not to stab her in the back? She'd confiscated that report but he could easily re-write it, give it to Jeremy Cadstock as ammunition for his crusade. What a prize idiot she'd been!

Worst of all, though, were her horrible suspicions that he'd planned to use his sexual power over her to lower her defences. Had he seduced her out of cold calculation, intended to use her in some despicable way and then betray her even more cruelly than he'd already done? This was the man she'd been planning to make her equal partner, in business as in life. Perhaps she should be congratulating herself on her lucky escape.

But it wasn't over yet, she reminded herself as she drove home. Grant could still be dangerous, more so if he bore her a grudge. Yet what else could she have done but sack him? Still tormenting herself with thoughts of what might have been and might still happen, Julia entered the haven of her flat and poured herself a stiff drink.

The *Healthy Life* piece arrived by second post and Julia settled down to read it, hoping it would take her mind off Grant. She soon realised that the article fell short of the anonymity and 'subtle suggestion' which the editor had guaranteed. The club was identifiable, for a start, thanks to a photo taken from the street which plainly showed the two buildings on either side of it. They hadn't actually used the name *Sybarites* but they'd spoken of the 'echoes of classical Greece' that the name evoked.

Then there was the passage describing the massage service.

'. . . *the male masseurs are all highly trained in the art of bringing sensual pleasure and "complete relaxation" to women's bodies. Here over-stressed career women can live out their fantasies of total self-indulgence under the expert caresses of handsome, non-demanding lovers. To help the fantasy along, the men are all named after Hollywood sex gods – Warren, Sylvester, Marlon . . .'*

Julia threw the paper aside in disgust. She'd been given to understand that a balanced article would be produced, covering all aspects of the club, but nearly all of it was about the massage service. The personal stuff they'd written on her was annoying, too.

'. . . *Jenny (not her real name) who runs the Women's Club has a touch of glamour about her, with her dark blonde hair, delicate bone structure, sparkling green eyes and a gorgeous figure. She runs her all-male staff with cool efficiency. The one question lurking in my mind was, does she ever use the massage service herself? When I asked her, she replied that it would be "unprofessional" to favour one masseur over another. So did she perhaps "favour" them all? I've got no answer to that one!'*

Before she could get too uptight about it, though, the phone rang. It was Phil, her accountant. 'Do you still want me to bid for that property on Wednesday?' he asked her.

Julia had forgotten that she'd asked him to attend the Millers auction. She hadn't wanted to be seen bidding in person, and Phil had agreed to do it for her. In the maelstrom of her confused feelings about Grant it had slipped her mind.

'Look, Phil, can I ring you back on this?' she asked him.

'Not having second thoughts are you, Julia?'

'I . . . I'm not sure. Can I ring you later?'

'Fine. I'll be in all evening.'

While Julia prepared herself a light meal that she didn't really want but felt she ought to eat, she tried to make up her mind about whether to expand her business. It seemed altogether the wrong time. If the rumours were to be believed, her existing club might soon be under threat of closure. Besides, her heart was no longer in it now she knew that Grant wasn't going to be manager. She had conceived of it as their joint project, something to set the seal on their relationship. Obviously she had seriously misjudged his character.

Yet something in her hated the idea of giving up on the project. It was a good idea, and it might prove to be her salvation if she ran it along the lines she'd discussed with Grant. No one could possibly object to a health club offering such options as yoga, herbalism and acupuncture. If it came to the crunch, it might offer her an insurance policy against total shutdown.

Besides, she mused, think what a coup it would be in Leo's eyes! She'd been looking forward to scotching his plan to turn the Millers site into an amusement arcade. It would be one in the eye for Grant, too, if she got it off the ground without him. Yes, she would like to show both men that she was capable of going it alone and making a success of it once again.

Picking up the phone, Julia rang Phil and told him to go ahead on Wednesday morning. He sounded pleased.

'You've got the backing, so you should go for it,' he told her. 'I'll do my best to secure the site, the rest is up to you.'

It was an echo of what had been said to her years

ago, when she set up *Sybarites*. She had succeeded then, and she would again. Feeling suddenly optimistic she phoned the magazine editor and told her answering machine that she should put the article on hold because there were new developments afoot which she might want to include. If her club was going to be identifiable she might as well make capital out of it by advertising her new venture. Maybe the whole article should be re-thought. With ideas buzzing in her head, Julia went to run herself a hot, deliciously scented bath.

Chapter Twelve

GRANT WAS GONE. Gone from the health club, and from Julia's sight, but not from her mind. There were so many heart-breaking reminders of his brief passage through her life. Every day, at work, she would either have to explain his departure to one of his former clients, or interview someone to replace him. The trouble was, no one could.

Then, when she returned home, it was far worse. Julia could just about tolerate the idea that she wasn't going to see him around the club any more, but the memories of him being in her flat were harder to quell. She couldn't take a shower without thinking about him, or make coffee, or sit on the sofa, or lie in her bed. And one night, when she was feeling particularly low, she discovered 'their' video in her bedroom drawer.

Julia knew it was foolish to try and watch it, but she couldn't resist the urge. Lying on her bed she flicked the remote control of her bedside screen and, as Grant's semi-naked body came into view, a great shuddering sigh went through her. She could remember it all, could still feel how every part of him had felt to her touch, especially the part that had delved in her innermost recesses to their mutual delight. It was agony watching him kiss her, strange feeling envious of the self she had been in that innocent, more hopeful time just weeks ago. Julia saw once more how her body awakened his desire, noticed the eager bulge in his G-string and, despite everything, felt proud that she had managed to satisfy him over and over again during that one, glorious weekend.

At least, she thought, I know what I'm capable of now.

Soon, though, Julia couldn't bear to just watch it any more. She closed her eyes. Another video was playing in her memory now, the one that had been acted out for real in this very room, just a short while ago. She delved beneath her blouse and found the sharp cones of her breasts, already bursting from her bra. Mimicking Grant's actions she pulled her taut flesh free of the restraining cups and began to finger her hot nipples. It wasn't enough. She stripped down to her pants and imagined herself being carried off into the bedroom by strong arms. The memory of his strip-tease made her moan softly with unfulfilled desire, and she tugged at her panties through which the wet stain of her lust was already seeping. Julia opened her eyes and glanced at the action on the screen. Oh God, now he was performing cunnilingus on her! What substitute could she find for those soft, liquid lips, that eager, probing tongue?

Julia opened her bedside cabinet and quickly sifted through the collection of ingenious gadgets she kept there for her personal use. She knew what she was looking for: It was a battery operated device that secreted an aphrodisiac cream through soft rubber 'lips' and provided the additional stimulation of a rhythmically probing 'tongue'. Julia held it to her vulva and switched it on, all the time watching what was happening on the screen. As the oral substitute set to work she tried to imagine that it was Grant's mouth down there, working its sensual magic. While her pussy was being thoroughly serviced, Julia fondled her straining breasts, trying to imitate Grant's subtle fingers. The simulation was only partly successful.

She closed her eyes, resurrecting the image of the lovemaking that had taken place on that very bed. Quickly Julia found a large dildo and placed the tip between her tumid lower lips, just as Grant had done, rubbing it gently against her clitoris. Slowly she inched it in, embracing the vibrator with her pelvic muscles as if it were Grant's beautiful penis. When it was in she threw the switch that made it throb with independent life, its cunningly placed profile giving extra stimulation to her engorged clitoris. Julia reached up to grasp her breasts with both hands, feeling what their ripe fullness had felt like to her lover, imagining the new dimension of desire they would have provoked in him.

The artificial penis was plunging into her now, half filling her vagina, but nowhere near as completely as Grant's fleshly organ had done. She opened her eyes again, seeing the dim pictures on the screen through a hazy veil of sultry passion. Watching his handsome head bend to her left nipple, Julia pushed her breast up to her mouth and found, with a brief cry of surprise, that she could just about lick the nipple herself. It had never occurred to her to try that before, and at first it felt weird, the alien texture of her own puckered flesh in her mouth. Soon, though, she found it exciting, flicking her tongue over each of her nipples in turn as she thrust her breasts up her chest as high as possible.

Down below she could feel the relentless

vibrations bringing her closer and closer to the edge of her resistance, the stimulating cream mingling with her natural secretions so that she was slick and juicy, making the dildo suck its way up and down her swollen passage. Closing her eyes once more, Julia found she could easily imagine that it was *his* body inside her, that vital extension of his most precious being penetrating her to the core. And the lips that teased rapidly across the tips of first one breast then the other could have been *his* lips, the hands that were filled with her bounteous bosom, *his* hands. And at the moment when the fantasy became complete, when Julia had really managed to conjure up his vital presence and fool her mind with her senses, she came.

The fierce contractions went on and on, almost painful in their intensity and blotting out her consciousness. When Julia regained her awareness a deep sadness enveloped her. She switched off the vibrator that had been expelled from her vagina and was still jerking around futiley on the bed, then flicked the switch to shut down the video. Stretching herself out face down on the duvet, she started weeping.

It was a different kind of release from her orgasm, the dismal recognition that fantasy was not real life and that although her body was thoroughly satiated her soul had been scarcely touched. Even so, she refused to feel ashamed of what she had just done, despite Grant's apparent disgust with her sex toys. It was thanks to them, she reckoned, that she had been so responsive when some real love-making had come her way. They'd kept her sexual machine ticking over. But now that love had gone what else could she do but resort to their help again?

Nor was she ashamed of her bout of self-pity. At night she was allowed to feel weak and vulnerable,

158

to sigh in the dark and weep into her pillow. It was the only way she could cope during the day. And she was coping, most of the time.

The plans for the holistic health centre progressed apace. Phil managed to acquire the Millers site for her, and his forward projections had been approved by the bank, so it was all systems go for the new club. Now that the financing was secured, Julia was caught up in discussing plans with the architect. It should have been fun, but she missed the input Grant would have provided. Although she was proud of her achievements, it would have been so much more exciting to have someone to share her enthusiasm, talk to someone who would add a new angle to her schemes.

Tentative enquiries amongst the local 'quacks' as Leo used to call them – the practitioners of complimentary health care – produced an encouraging response. In return for good facilities most were willing to work at the new club at least one morning or afternoon a week. There was no shortage of people willing to run classes, either.

Then, one evening, Leo rang.

'So, you pipped me at the post for the Millers site,' he began. 'Shame you didn't have the guts to do it in person, Julia. I recognised that weaselly accountant of yours at once.'

'I had no time to attend the auction,' she lied. 'Anyway, I suppose you know all about my plans now, through the grapevine?'

'I've heard a few rumours,' he admitted grudgingly. 'I hope you've got reliable finance, though. You paid well over the odds for that tip heap.'

'If you mean that prime location convenient to my present business premises, then I have to disagree,' she countered, smiling to herself.

'So, what *are* you going to do with it. Open a

brothel?'

'Don't be childish, Leo. And if your spy system hasn't come up with the information yet, far be it from me to tell you. You'll have to wait and see, like everyone else.'

She was enjoying this! Beneath Leo's urbane manner she knew he was as mad as hell – and burning with curiosity.

'I'll find out soon enough. But a word of warning, cherub. It had better not be anything remotely improper. Not with a certain person breathing fire and brimstone down everyone's necks. Word has it that he's about to come clean about his plans for this town, and "clean" is the operative word!'

'I'll cross that particular bridge when I come to it,' she answered, more confidently than she felt.

'Well don't forget, my sweet, if there's anything I can do . . .'

'Thanks, Leo. I'll let you know.'

'I enjoyed our little tête à tête the other week, by the way. Sorry if I overstepped the mark a bit. I could say it was the old hooch, but I think it had more to do with you still being a damned attractive woman and me continuing to be a red-blooded male. Anyway, I hope we can do it again sometime.'

'Maybe, Leo. Well, thanks for ringing.'

Julia always felt uneasy after speaking to her ex-husband, and tonight was no exception. He was playing some sort of game with her, he always was. Not for nothing was he in the gambling business – it suited his mentality. Still, she wasn't going to waste too much time and energy speculating on the motives of someone she'd shut out of her life a long time ago.

The editor of *Healthy Life* was very interested in the idea of expanding the article to include Julia's plans for the new club. It fitted in with her policy of including news of alternative therapies in the magazine. She agreed to defer publication of the article until the new year, much to Julia's relief. She had enough to deal with at the moment.

Keeping busy, busy, busy . . . that was the way Julia dealt with the hidden wound left by Grant's betrayal. She managed eventually to find a replacement masseur, 'Arnie', with a body that was almost a match for his namesake, and his clients seemed to love him. It was almost, Julia thought ruefully, as if Grant had never existed.

Above all she was glad, now, that she'd gone ahead with the new club. There was so much to do that the days went by in a whirl and Julia was so tired at night, after a swim and a workout, that she had no difficulty getting to sleep. If her dreams were troubled, she didn't remember them. And sex, for her, was a thing of the past. She'd thrown out all her toys, never watched the video screens unless she had to, ignored the old yearning if it occurred. All of her time, thought and energy was directed towards making a success of the new club, which she had christened the *Holistic Health Club*.

Then, one Friday morning, Julia opened her copy of the *Gazette* and her world came tumbling down.

The headline screamed at her: *MP's Plan for Clean-Up*. She knew at once what it was about, but Jeremy Cadstock was quoted as saying,

'There are, in this town, certain unsavoury establishments going under the name of Sporting Clubs, Discos, Health Clubs and the like, which are little more than fronts for gambling, drugs and prostitution. I am urging the council to scrutinise their activities very closely before renewing the licences for such premises.'

Julia thought his language, with its oddly dated ring, made him sound like some small-town mayor in a Hollywood film about the Prohibition era.

Nevertheless, it struck a chill into her. If the man had actually tapped a latent vein of Puritanism in the public there would be no stopping him.

She went into the club that day in a mood of trepidation. Steven was actually reading a copy of the paper as she approached his desk.

'Bad news eh, Miss Julia?' He grimaced. 'What do you make of it all, then?'

'Could be a storm in a teacup,' she ventured bravely.

'Er . . . pardon my asking, but when *is* our licence up for renewal?'

'Not for another four weeks. Hopefully this will all have blown over by then.'

Steven's face lightened a little. He leaned towards her and said, under his breath, 'Maybe the fact that Mrs You-know-who is a member will count in our favour, if you know what I mean.'

Julia sighed, remembering that Doreen had been conspicuous by her absence since Grant had left. 'I wish life were that simple! But you may be right. At the moment we can only wait and see, can't we?'

During the following week, however, it became increasingly obvious that morale had been affected by the 'Cadstock Clean-up Campaign', or 'CCC' as it was now called. Every time she went into the staff restroom, or visited the pool or gym, she found dismal-faced employees, often in huddles, gloomily discussing their prospects. When Steven reported that everyone was feeling very insecure, Julia confessed that she just didn't know what to do about it.

'How about a pep talk?' he suggested. 'Get everyone together and let them know you intend to fight in our corner. You've got some influence on the council, haven't you?'

'Not much,' Julia admitted. Even so, the idea of

holding a staff meeting seemed a good one and she promised to give it some thought.

Then came an unexpected bonus, in the shapely form of Rebecca Maitland. She and Lou came to see Julia in her office one morning.

'I hope you won't think that we're poking our nose in where we're not wanted,' Rebecca began, rather nervously. 'But we really like this club and we want to do something to show our support.'

'Support?'

'Yes, over this CCC business. We're very worried that *Sybarites* might get closed down.'

Julia suppressed an impatient sigh. 'Thank you for your concern, but . . .'

'So we've decided to get up a petition,' Lou broke in firmly. 'With your permission, of course. We want to get as many influential local women to sign up as possible.'

Julia couldn't help laughing a little. 'You mean you want women to put their names to a petition to save *Sybarites*? I think that's highly unlikely. Most of our members come here because I can guarantee them privacy, anonymity. They'd never publicly admit to being members.'

'I think you'd be surprised,' Rebecca smiled. 'Maybe some of the older women would be shy about it, but most of the younger members wouldn't mind at all. There's me and Lou, for a start, and six of our friends have promised to sign – two of them are members. And I'm sure we could get more.'

It was an intriguing idea. A show of public confidence could be just what was needed to boost staff morale and persuade the council in their favour.

'All right,' Julia smiled. 'See what you can do. I'll get Steven to run off some forms and you can take them out and about. If it comes to nothing then at least you'll have tried. And I'm very grateful that you care enough to bother.'

'We think there should be more places like this, just for women,' Lou said.

Julia thought of telling them about the new club, then decided against it for the moment. But she did invite them to the staff meeting she was holding in three days time, when she intended to announce her plans for the *Holistic Health Club*.

For a moment, as the two girls sat smiling before her, Julia was reminded of their massage session with Grant and her brighter mood faded. They had both booked (separate) sessions with Arnie, the new masseur. She hoped they wouldn't be disappointed.

The day before the staff meeting on Friday, Julia decided to attend Jeremy Cadstock's surgery. It was a calculated risk, but she needed to find out more about his intentions before she spoke to her staff. She'd never had any direct dealings with him before and found she was shaking, with sweaty palms, as she sat in the waiting room with another man.

At last it was her turn. The MP rose with a practised smile as she entered the room, offering her a limp hand. He was a tall, thin man in his late fifties, with thin greying hair and quick brown eyes that darted all over her, like a foraging insect, before settling on her face.

'Julia Marquis, owner of *Sybarites* Health Club,' she introduced herself.

'Ah, Miss Marquis! I've heard of you. Met your ex-husband, Leo. Do sit down.'

His manner was non-committal but she knew he was preparing himself, writing his script in advance. Well, she had the advantage over him. She'd been thinking about what to say for days.

'Mr Cadstock, I'll come straight to the point. You've been talking recently about "scrutinising" the activities of health clubs in this town . . .'

'Not personally, I can assure you. I merely urged the licensing committee to be more vigilant when renewing club licences.'

'But you intend to put pressure on them to close down what you call "unsavoury establishments". Isn't that right?'

'Absolutely. And I believe I'm acting in the best interests of the citizens of this town, indeed of the country. You might be surprised at the volume of support I've had since I started my "Clean-Up" Campaign. The letters keep rolling in, ninety per cent of them on my side. It's most encouraging.' He gave her a lukewarm smile.

Julia decided to play her trump card.

'I wonder if you're aware that your wife is a member of my club?'

His smile wavered just a little. 'An *ex*-member, I think you'll find Miss Marquis. There were certain aspects of your . . . services that she found distasteful. I have evidence that your . . . "masseurs" are . . . indulging in unethical practices. Naturally, I shall be advising the licensing committee accordingly.'

Julia swallowed her rage. 'I'm sure they will find nothing grossly untoward going on. The vast majority of our members are completely satisfied with the facilities and services we provide.'

'We shall see, shan't we? And now, if you've no more points to raise, I must ask you to excuse me. I have a meeting to attend on the other side of town.'

Julia took the feeble hand again, seething inside. How she would have loved to mention Tanya Wentworth! But she didn't dare. It was likely that the politician would have worked out a cover for his relationship with her years ago and now was not the time to challenge him.

Once she was in her car and driving home, Julia reflected grimly on what Cadstock had said about having 'evidence'. Was he referring to the report Grant had made for Doreen? Or had Tanya told him anything? She'd certainly had more first-hand experience. Either way, it sounded bad. If he went to the council with his story they might feel obliged to make some kind of official inspection, which could prove both embarrassing and, ultimately, fatal to *Sybarites*.

To counteract the threat Julia would have to get support from as many councillors as possible. She knew she could count on three of the licensing committee putting in a good word for her, as they had wives or girlfriends who were members.

Then there was Leo. His friend the police inspector had always been sympathetic, although whether he would actually use his influence on her behalf was doubtful. Perhaps she should phone Leo and talk to him about the latest developments. After all, he had offered to help.

That evening she gave him a call. He sounded less than pleased to hear her voice but it soon turned out that he had troubles of his own.

'Damned interfering sod! He's got it in for gamblers, now!' he moaned. Julia couldn't help smirking a little. Leo had been so keen to warn *her* that he'd forgotten his own business was equally vulnerable. Still, it was no joke really.

'What about your policeman friend?' she suggested. 'Can't he do anything?'

'I doubt it. Not up front, anyway. Got to keep his nose very clean these days. Still, I'll certainly have a chat with him about it. And I'd advise you to do what I said, Julia. Make sure your masseurs get their act squeaky clean. At least till the heat's off.'

'I'm sure you're right, Leo. Well, thanks. And let's

keep in touch, shall we? If either of us hears anything we'll keep each other informed. Okay?'

'You know, it's funny really, you and I. After all we've been through we've never really co-operated until now. Now we're under threat. Just like the war, really. Ah well.'

Julia let his last, enigmatic remark go, and put down the phone. Much as she had disliked and distrusted Leo in the past it was nice to have someone to talk to in her hour of need.

It should have been Grant, she thought. But maybe it was Grant who had got her into this mess. The confused feelings that always assailed her when she thought about him resurfaced. What if he'd been directly in league with Jeremy Cadstock all along, and that revenge story about Doreen and Tanya had been a complete fabrication? It was possible she would never know the truth now.

When the time came for her to face her assembled staff, Julia felt extremely nervous. It seemed she had little in the way of good news to tell them, after all. They were waiting for her in the Healthfood Bar, some with drinks in front of them, and as she entered they gave her a brief and rather self-conscious round of applause. Looking round, it struck her what a very healthy and good-looking bunch they were. Rebecca and Lou were there too, dressed in casual, almost sloppy clothes that belied their profession.

'Well, we don't often get together like this, do we?' she began. 'It's a shame the occasion is not a happier one. As most of you know, *Sybarites* seems to be under threat from this new campaign to clear up the town. Now I don't know how urgent a threat this is as yet, but we'd foolish not to take it seriously. I went to see Mr Cadstock, and it seems he has some kind of "evidence" to bring before the council.'

There was a brief hubbub, during which Doreen's

name was circulated. Fortunately, no one mentioned Grant.

Rebecca cleared her throat nervously and caught Julia's eye. 'Can I say something, please?' Julia nodded. 'Well, we've got up this petition . . .' She waved a bundle of forms at them, 'and so far the response has been very good. Lou and I have got twenty-five signatures already!'

'That's excellent! Well done!' Julia beamed. At last she could inject a note of optimism into the proceedings.

'It's to say that women want the club kept open and they like the way it's run,' Lou explained hastily. 'Several women with their own business have signed it . . .'

'Including Pam Styles from *The Body Beautiful*,' Rebecca put in.

'And there's even a couple of men.'

'Husbands!' Rebecca said, making the men in the room laugh.

When the room had quietened, Julia spoke more gravely. 'This is marvellous, and I don't mean to undermine what you two have done, but I'm afraid it may not be enough. What I've decided is this. For the time being, until we're sure that this has blown over, I'm going to insist that you give straight massages only.'

There was a subdued outcry. The loudest protesters were the two girls. Julia held up her hand for silence before continuing. 'Look, it's only temporary. But there may be some sort of spot-check on the way and I don't want us to be caught out.'

Rebecca spoke up. 'But isn't that against your principles? Shouldn't you be standing up for the rights of women instead of giving in to this kind of puritanical pressure?'

Julia sighed. 'I'm concerned, first and foremost, about staying in business. I can't do anything if *Sybarites* closes. This is crisis management, and this measure is, as I said, only short term. We can think about fighting for our rights when the climate is more favourable. Right now, I'm not really sure how much support this Clean-up Campaign has amongst local people, so I'm erring on the side of caution.'

Everyone looked downcast, so Julia decided to tell them the good news.

'However, there is something to look forward to *if* we survive. I have plans to open another club.' Ripples of pleased surprise spread round the room. 'It will be different from this one, more concerned with women's health matters, but I intend to link the two clubs. Membership will automatically be for both. So you see, not only is this club in jeopardy if Mr Cadstock has his way, but possibly the new club as well.'

'We'll get more signatures,' Lou declared. Then, turning to the men, she added, 'If any of you would like to take a petition form there are plenty more here. Ask all the women you know to sign.'

'And plenty you don't know, too!' Rebecca added, with a grin.

Julia came out of the meeting feeling she had her staff on her side. Several came up to offer their support, and Steve commented that 'that cad Cadstock has got a fight on his hands!'

Yet there was a bleakness in her heart, partly because she'd had to take Leo's advice. It had been a painful decision to make, restricting her massage service, but she knew Leo was right and she couldn't take any risks. Of course, if Cadstock already had his evidence no amount of window-dressing would convince the council that the club was respectable. But this was an exercise in damage

169

limitation that might, just, come off if she kept her cool.

That was difficult to do whenever she thought of Grant. If he was behind this witch-hunt she would never, never forgive him. It was tempting to do something really hurtful, such as sending some candid shots of his massages of Doreen and Tanya to the *Gazette*, to show just what Cadstock's two women liked to have done to them in their spare time. She even had footage of the two women in the sauna. Perhaps a hint to the Honourable Member . . .?

No, Julia decided, it was too early to play such a dangerous game. It might backfire on her badly, since the massages had taken place on her premises. For the time being they would just have to keep their collective nose clean and see what happened.

Chapter Thirteen

JULIA AWOKE IN the middle of the night, disturbed by a dream. As the details returned to her through the veil of sleep, she blushed to remember it.

Grant (of course, it had to be him!) had her pinioned face down on the bed and he was slapping her bottom, hard. She knew he was acting in anger for not trusting him, not believing his story. Suddenly rough hands grasped her round the waist and hoisted her up on to her knees. He thrust her thighs apart and then she felt him pushing his way into her from behind, not as before but this time sneaking in between her buttocks. Julia felt herself stretching painfully to accommodate his turgid penis until he was fully inside her, probing into her secret shame, making her grunt as she gained some bestial gratification from the act. When her humiliation was complete, and he'd made her come by fingering her clitoris, he pulled out and lay prostrate on top of her, pushing the very breath out of her body with his weight, stifling her voice so that she couldn't even call out to him to save herself. It was at that point that panic had set in and she'd woken up.

The feelings that the dream aroused in Julia were

obscurely masochistic, related to how she'd felt when Grant had discovered her voyeuristic and masturbatory secrets. It also reflected the way she now felt about the sex they'd shared, which had become polluted in retrospect by his treachery. A briefly-recovered innocence had been shattered, hope had been banished and trust broken, leaving profound disillusionment.

For the whole day the atmosphere of the dream lingered on, subtly corrupting everything she saw around her. Checking on the masseurs through the video, Julia found their careful avoidance of stimulating their clients more lewd than their former frank sex play. The club members had been told of the new arrangements and most of them accepted it as a temporary necessity, but a few had tried to make their masseurs behave in the old way.

Julia watched with a frown as one woman snatched at Marlon's hand and thrust it between her thighs, writhing and moaning. He had drawn back, explained why he wasn't allowed to touch her there for the time being, and she had reluctantly settled for a foot massage which, by means of her squeezing her thighs together throughout in rhythmical fashion, had apparently proved satisfactory. Another client had actually offered Arnie money to satisfy her, but despite being new to the job he had declined and talked her into accepting a normal massage.

A few members had been so disgruntled that they'd threatened to resign. By the end of the day Julia had had to mollify three frustrated women, promising that normal service would be resumed as soon as possible and urging them to sign the petition if they'd not already done so. There were now over fifty signatures and Julia decided to tell Alan Bond, her best friend on the council, that she intended to present the petition at their licensing meeting. When she rang he listened politely, but warned her that the mood of the committee was turning in Jeremy Cadstock's favour.

'The public seem to be behind him,' he explained. 'But the tide could well turn again over the next couple of weeks. I'll keep you informed anyway, Julia.'

It was the best she could hope for at that juncture, but as she returned home that evening Julia felt defeated. Her plans for the new club were beginning to seem like an excursion into cloud-cuckoo land.

Worst of all, though, she found herself thinking constantly about Grant, wondering what he was doing, whether he was regretting his folly, missing her even. There had been no request for references. Bleakly, Julia wondered if he had gone back on the boats. It would be the obvious way out, since that way he could by-pass her reference. And running away to sea was what he'd resorted to before when he'd needed to forget a woman. Yes, she concluded, that was the most likely reason why she hadn't seen him around.

That didn't stop her scanning every passing face as she drove along. What would she do if she saw him with another woman? What if the other woman turned out to be someone she knew: Rebecca or Lou, for example, or even Tanya Wentworth? Had there been yet another hidden agenda at work in the tangled web woven by Grant Delaney, one that involved a further betrayal? Torture though it was to think of it, Julia now felt she wouldn't put anything past him.

Once she got home, the local evening news didn't help improve Julia's jaundiced mood.

'Jeremy Cadstock's Clean-up Campaign is gathering momentum,' said the woman newscaster smugly, as Julia watched the TV over a bowl of pasta. 'Four councillors have come out in support of his move to close down certain clubs in the area, which he describes as "gross and ugly warts on the otherwise pleasant face of this town". The first of the licences to come up for renewal is *Chancers' Casino* in Queen Street. The Licensing Committee are meeting to discuss this next Tuesday. Several bodies, including the Licensed Victuallers' Association, are regarding this as a test case . . .'

Julia sat, horrified, through the news item then switched off the television and picked up the phone. It was almost a reflex action. The casino was one that Leo had a share in and she felt she had to offer him some support. When he answered, it was obvious from the thickness of his voice that he'd already been drinking.

'Jules, how delightful, how charming of you to ring, my dear!'

'I just saw the local news. I'm so sorry, Leo. Apparently *Chancers'* licence is to be reviewed under this ridiculous clean-up campaign.'

'Knew that all along, sweetie. Been doing my homework, see? That place ain't called "Chancers" for nothing, eh? But have I got news for you! Must tell you. Not over the phone, though. Can I come round?'

'Well . . .'

'Not for long, just for a chat. We said we'd keep in touch, didn't we, and pass on any little titbits? I'm sure you'll want to hear what I've found out.'

'Okay,' she agreed reluctantly. Already Julia was regretting having picked up the phone, but if he really did have something important to tell her she couldn't afford to let it go. It was obvious that the pace of the campaign was hotting up dangerously, and soon the fate of *Sybarites* would be on the line.

Leo arrived half an hour later, visibly the worse for drink. His cheeks, always on the florid side, were flushed bright red and his yellow-green eyes looked unnaturally bright. Julia sat him down and brewed a couple of espresso coffees. Leo insisted on pouring a generous measure of brandy into his.

'Terrible mess all this. That Cadstock chap should be court-marshalled, or whatever they do with MPs who overstep the mark!'

'I don't think there's any danger of him losing his seat,' she remarked wryly. 'If anything, he's more popular than ever with the locals. At least, according to the media.'

Leo waved an impatient hand. 'You surely don't believe everything those wallies say, do you my dear? Come on, you're smarter than that!'

He held out his hand, wanting her to sit beside him on the sofa, but in order to escape him Julia went into the kitchen to make more coffee. The thought of sitting on *that* sofa with Leo was distasteful to her. Already she had the feeling she'd made a mistake inviting him to her flat. He looked well ensconced, and it would be hard to shift him.

When Julia returned with the coffee jug she said briskly, 'Now then, Leo, you said you had something to tell me. What is it?'

He gave her a conspiratorial grin. 'It's about Cadstock's floosie. You're going to love this. Guess what – that Wentworth woman went to school with his wife, the delectable Doreen! They're best friends, so my informant tells me. What's going on then, eh? Maybe they go in for threesomes. Wouldn't that be a scoop for the old *Gazette*?'

Julia threw him a weary glance. 'Is that it?'

'What d'you mean, "Is that it?" '

'I mean, if that's all you've got to tell me then you're wasting my time. I already know about the relationship between Tanya and Doreen. They both belong to the club – or used to.'

'Do they?' He spun round in his seat, clearly excited. 'Doesn't say much for the old cuckold's sexual prowess then, does it, if both his wife and his mistress have to get their jollies elsewhere!' He chuckled. 'Couldn't you get some stuff on 'em, old girl? Slip a few photos to a reporter or something? If we can destroy the Cad's credibility we're halfway home and dry.'

'It's not as simple as that, Leo. I can't very well make their membership of *Sybarites* public without saying why it's significant. Most people think it's just a health club.'

'Hah! Well don't say I didn't warn you!'

Julia checked her irritation as best she could, putting on an ironic 'little wifey' voice. 'Well, what do you suggest I do, Leo dear? Since you're the expert in these matters.'

'I told you, try to get the Cad hoist with his own petard. Most people don't even know he's got a mistress. I should think the *Gazette* would be very interested to know her identity.'

'I'm not sure that's enough on its own. I mean, all he has to do is deny it. You know how often politicians get away with that sort of thing. As long as the woman herself keeps her mouth shut and there are no children involved it's hard to prove. And those two have had several years of practice at keeping a low profile.'

'I suppose I could get old Josh on the case . . .'

Julia perched on the sofa cushion for an instant, placing a restraining hand on his arm.

'No, Leo, please don't involve him. I'm sure that's not the way to play this. We must get public opinion on our side or we haven't a hope. Two of my members have got up a petition . . .'

Leo gave a sudden snort. 'Yeah, I heard about that! You really think that's going to do any good?'

Julia shrugged. He'd hit a raw nerve. She'd had her doubts about the worth of such a gesture from the start, seeing it as more of a morale booster for the club members and staff than a serious threat to the campaign.

'Maybe, maybe not. But I don't want to get involved in anything scandalous, not right now. Don't you see how awkward the timing is for me, now that I'm planning this new venture. I don't want to put both clubs in jeopardy.'

Leo placed a clumsy hand on her knee. 'Oh dear, oh dear, oh dear! We have made a mess of things, haven't we?'

'Say what you mean, Leo.'

'I mean, old bean, that you bit off a bit more than you can chew when you threw the old lion out and tried to go it alone.'

'Don't be so ridiculous! If you're going to be insulting . . .'

'I did warn you, cherub. I said you were making a mistake by turning the club into a women-only massage parlour. Too sleazy by half.'

Julia was exasperated. Leo had come to her flat on the pretext of offering her some kind of help but all he was really interested in was crowing over her. Still, she knew it was no use arguing with him in his present mood.

'Got any more of this lovely brandy?' Leo looked at her, red-eyed.

She shook her head, remembering from the old days that when he'd had too much to drink he became uncontrollably randy.

Leo staggered to his feet and pulled her up beside him, staring at her. The expression on his face was a ludicrous travesty of tenderness, like a pantomime

177

actor trying to show larger-than-life emotions. Julia hated him when he got like this. It brought back memories of nights spent lying under him, feeling nothing, while he huffed and puffed away towards his own feeble climax then turned over and went to sleep, ignoring her needs.

'Come on, Jules,' he cajoled, his voice thick and plummy. 'You and me, we should stick together on this, help each other. Neither of us are much good on our own, are we? Let's drink a toast, to the good times ahead. 'Cos together we'll win through, you bet your sweet life we will! Where's that brandy?'

He lurched away then turned back towards her, grabbed her by the arm and thrust his grotesque face into hers. Unable to wriggle from his grip, she tried nevertheless to back away.

'Come on, babe, let me see those great big beautiful boobs of yours!' he leered. To Julia's horror he began pawing at her pink angora cardigan with his free hand, clumsily attacking the dainty pearl buttons. Underneath she wore only a bra. Now she remembered how it felt to be truly vulnerable, to have her mind and soul as well as her body mastered by sheer force of will, and she began to loathe her ex-husband all over again.

Knowing that she mustn't show her feelings, she tried to speak reasonably to him. 'Leave me alone please, Leo. We're not married now, remember? If you've said all you had to say I'll phone for a taxi to take you home. You're in no fit state to drive.'

'Let me stay the night then. I promise to be good, if you give me one look at those lovely tits. They used to be mine, after all. All mine . . .'

Again Julia tried to struggle free of his grasp but he summoned up his strength and pulled at the front of her cardigan, making the flimsy buttons pop open. Her heart was beating wildly as she twisted and turned, trying to get away so that she could lock herself in the bathroom. In desperation Julia evolved a plan. She would crawl through the bathroom window on to the balcony outside and then down the fire escape ladder.

But Leo's great paws were pulling at her bra, ripping down the straps and pulling down the cups to expose her breasts. The memory of a thousand similar assaults revived themselves in her mind, weakening her resolve. What was the use? Leo had always had his way with her, whether by guile, wheedling or brute force. The fact that she'd divorced him counted for nothing in the ongoing interplay of their wills. She'd believed that she had forged a new identity for herself. Well, he was showing her that she was wrong, that was all. At heart, Julia knew she was the same cowed creature she had always been.

He was slobbering over her breasts now, like a spoilt, overfed child. Disgusted, Julia seized a handful of his thinning hair and jerked his head back from her chafed nipple.

'No, Leo! I don't belong to you any more.'

His manner suddenly changed. The hazel eyes, still red-tinged, grew narrow and mean.

'Who do you belong to, then? Is there anyone else? Tell me, Jules, I want to know. Have you found someone else?'

Seeing this as perhaps a more sure escape route than the bathroom, Julia nodded dumbly.

'Who is he? Do I know him?' Leo's stinking breath was nauseating. She tried to turn her face away but he held her head firmly in place. 'Tell me! I want to know!'

'He . . . he's someone I met at the club. No, you don't know him. Actually . . .' Julia improvised, in desperation. 'Actually, I'm expecting him any minute now. He said he'd come round . . .'

Leo gave her a disbelieving grin. 'Oh yeah? Any minute now, eh? Well, I'd like to meet this lover boy of yours so I think I'll stick around.'

'No, Leo! Please! Look, I can phone for a taxi.'

Without answering, he took both her exposed breasts in his hands and raised them in turn to his slobbery lips. Julia was near to tears. How long must she endure this? Now there was only the bathroom, and her alternative plan of escape. She glanced towards the door in the corridor. It seemed a long way off.

'Best thing about your body, your gorgeous boobs,' Leo was saying, nipping her painfully with his teeth. 'I married you for your tits, do you know that? Had to have them all to myself, see. Didn't want anyone else pawing them about.'

Julia didn't like the turn his 'conversation' was taking. There was a definite risk of him working himself up into a jealous fury over her imaginary lover. Maybe inventing him hadn't been such a good idea, after all.

She tried pleading with him. 'Look, Leo, you said you only wanted a little look and now you've had that. So will you please leave me alone and let me call a cab? I'm tired and I want to go to bed.'

'Hah!' He pounced on her mistake at once, proving he was not as drunk as she'd thought. 'Going to bed, eh? What, without lover boy?'

'I mean, when he arrives.'

'No you didn't, sweetie. But since you've mentioned it, how about going to bed with me instead? For old time's sake. I think that would be rather nice, don't you?'

'No I don't, Leo, and please stop doing that!'

'Come on, let me undress you. Be my little dolly, remember? We used to play that game.'

180

Julia tried being firm with him. She managed to slip from his grasp and stepped away for a few moments. 'No, Leo. We're not playing that game any more.'

He lunged at her, pulling at her waistband, and before she could stop him he was unzipping her jeans. She slapped his hand, but he began to yank the jeans down over her hips, exposing her panties.

'Mm, black lace ones!' he grinned, salivating. 'My favourite!'

She tried her last, desperate ploy. 'No stop this! My boyfriend will be here any moment!'

He leered up at her, his face level with her crotch. 'Sorry, darling, that one won't wash any more. I know there's no boyfriend. You know there's no boyfriend. No knight in shining armour coming to rescue you this time.'

But then she heard it. At first, Julia thought she must be hallucinating, but then it came again, the sound of the doorbell, shriller than before.

'There you are!' she snapped at him. 'Someone at the door!'

He laughed. 'Your boyfriend, is it? I think not. Probably someone trying to sell something. Wait here, I'll answer it.'

Julia had wanted to get there first, to plead for help, make her escape, anything. But Leo was too quick for her. As she followed him out into the hall he was already opening the door. Aware of her dishevelled state, with her breasts exposed and her jeans around her knees, Julia was about to hide in the bathroom when a deep voice said, 'Oh, good evening. Is Julia in?'

Transfixed she stared into the black hole of the doorway. Leo had stepped back a litte, nonplussed by the sudden appearance of this stranger and befuddled by drink, allowing Julia a good look at the caller. Not that she needed to. That rich, mellow voice was unmistakable.

'Grant!'

'Julia!'

As she stared at him she saw his face undergo a terrible metamorphosis. The warm smile faded, the eyes turned from the friendly blue of a summer sky into the leaden grey of a winter sea, and his jaw set like an ominously jutting rock. Twisting his beautiful mouth into an ugly leer he snarled, 'And what the hell has been going on here?'

Chapter Fourteen

JULIA GAPED AT him, wanting to sink into the aquamarine sea of her hall carpet. Grant's burning gaze made her aware of her bare breasts and she tugged the remnants of her cardigan over them then realised she had no free hand to pull up the zip of her jeans. Absurdly, she fell back on protocol.

'Er . . . Grant, this is Leo, my ex-husband. He . . . er . . . came round as I was getting ready to have a shower.'

Julia knew how ridiculous she was sounding, making the situation ten times worse. The two men glowered at each other, Leo through rheumy, drink-sodden eyes and Grant through ominously sober ones.

'So this is your new boyfriend, Julia,' Leo began, offering Grant a feeble hand, which he ignored. 'So pleased to meet you. Glad to know she's found someone else at last . . .'

'Leo!' Julia said, sharply. 'I think it's probably time you went. I'll ring for a taxi.'

She had a few blessed minutes of relief as the two men went through to the sitting-room and she picked up the hall phone. The taxi firm promised to send a cab within five minutes. Thankfully Julia sneaked into the bathroom, locked the door and stood with her back against it, taking deep breaths. She knew she was being cowardly but she just couldn't face either man right now. Whatever Grant wanted could wait until Leo was safely dispatched.

But why *had* he called round? Julia's heartbeat was only just stabilising after the shock of seeing him there in her doorway. Scarcely a day had gone by since his dismissal when she hadn't conjured up his image, but all the power of her imagination hadn't been able to do him justice. She'd forgotten just how good-looking he was, how dark and glossy his hair, how his eyes glinted like sapphires in sunlight, how velvetly seductive his voice even when, as tonight, he was angry. Then there were the indefinable things, the elusive scent of him that no amount of manufactured cologne could hide, the aura of vitality that surrounded him, the way his body moved with lithe grace beneath his clothes.

Moving towards the mirror she did her best to make herself more presentable, combing her hair and spraying mineral water on her cheeks to freshen up. Then she squirted some *Amarige* down her cleavage to boost her shattered morale, did her buttons up properly and emerged from the bathroom just as the doorbell was ringing.

'I'll get it!' she called, as Leo lurched into view.

'Nice fella,' Leo commented on his way out. 'Worked as a croupier once. I might have a job for him . . .'

Julia ushered her ex through the door with great relief. Well, Grant, you're full of surprises, she thought, as she faced the door to the sitting-room. Not least of which was his appearance at her flat that evening. Whatever had prompted his visit, she had to admit he had perfect timing.

When she entered the room Grant was standing

184

thoughtfully by the fireplace, a brandy glass beside him on the mantelpiece. KD Lang was singing a soulful ditty on the CD player. Julia expected a smile from him, but his face remained stern as he surveyed her.

The hurt he'd done to her throbbed angrily, like a re-opened scar. Who the hell does he think he is, she asked herself. If he'd come to gloat she would show him the door.

'Hullo, Julia, I'm sorry if I called at an awkward time.' His tone was an uneasy attempt at sardonic.

'You came in the nick of time, actually.' Julia passed in front of him on her way to the drinks cabinet, poured herself a brandy and returned to face him. 'Although anyone would have been a welcome diversion from Leo in his cups. He tends to get a bit . . . overbearing.'

'Oh yeah? Is that why you were so obviously ready for bed when I arrived?'

'Grant, you surely don't think . . . oh yes, I suppose you do. Look, he started pulling the clothes off me, right? He was drunk, as you saw, but he wouldn't have got any further, not if I could help it. There's nothing between me and Leo . . . hell, why do I sound like I'm making excuses? I don't owe you any explanation. I don't owe you anything!'

Despite herself, she was secretly pleased by Grant's obvious jealousy.

'You're right, and I'm sorry. It was a bit of a shock, that's all. I mean, after what we'd shared . . .'

They were regarding each other like wary beasts. Their weekend of unfettered passion was the unspoken bond that neither wanted to acknowledge openly.

Julia waited for more from him but Grant remained silent, so she said coolly. 'Was this just a social call? Business?' She couldn't resist the cruel dig. 'Surely not pleasure?'

'To tell you the truth, I'm not sure why I'm here.'

Julia raised a quizzical eyebrow at him. Now the incident with Leo was over she felt more confident, in control. The weeks of telling herself that Grant was not worth bothering about were paying off.

She decided to confront him with her suspicions. After all, she had little to lose now. 'You heard the latest, I presume? About the threat to *Sybarites*? No doubt you've told Doreen about my future plans too, just to make sure I go out of business completely.'

He frowned, outraged. 'For heaven's sake, Julia, do you really think that's what I want?'

She shrugged. 'It doesn't matter what I think, does it? The damage is already done.'

Rough hands seized her by the shoulders before she knew what was happening. Grant's eyes blazed down at her. 'You silly bitch! Why can't you believe that I'm on your side? Ever since you sacked me I've been trying my damnedest to make amends. I even went to see Cadstock myself.'

'You what?'

'I went to one of his surgeries, tried to find out what was in his mind.'

'You did? That's incredible. I went to see him as well!'

For the first time that evening Grant's irresistible smile returned, though only fleetingly. 'There, you see? We're still on the same wavelength! So what did you discover?'

He let her go, sitting down on the sofa with his glass in his hand, just as he had last time he was in her flat. Julia stifled the memory.

'Not a lot. Only that he definitely has it in for my club. Doreen's resigned, of course, to cover herself. I don't know about Tanya.'

186

'I do.' Grant sounded quite excited. 'She's lying low, staying with a friend in the country until it all blows over. That means she and Cadstock are running scared.'

'You think so?'

'Definitely.' He grinned. 'Maybe now's the time to put the frighteners on him a bit more.'

Julia couldn't help laughing. 'Grant, you're sounding like a hoodlum in a Hollywood gangster movie!'

He pulled her down on to the sofa beside him. 'That's better. I've missed your smile, Julia. Amongst other things.'

She drew back, fighting the urge to sink into his arms and luxuriate in his warm, sexy body. Nothing could alter the fact that he'd almost betrayed her. She had the proof locked in her office safe, in the form of his wretched report.

'I thought I'd severed all ties with you, Grant,' she said. 'Both business and personal.'

He turned and faced her, gravely. 'I just want to do what I can to help. And I have an idea.'

'Yes?'

'It's about those videos.'

'Oh!'

'Okay, I'm sorry. I had no right to go on at you the way I did. I don't really know why I said those things. I was acting completely out of character. I see nothing wrong in people getting turned on by videos, or anything else.'

Julia sighed. 'I think you may have been wanting to get back at me, because you'd been found out.'

'You're probably right. Anyway, I've been thinking about the fact that you've got videos of me with clients. Particularly Doreen and Tanya . . .'

Julia held up a warning hand. 'If you're going to suggest blackmail, I've already dismissed it. Those

187

videos show exactly what I don't want the likes of Jeremy Cadstock to see. I daren't use them. I can't risk it.'

Grant looked thoughtful. Kind of like a brooding Greek god, Julia thought before she mentally reprimanded herself.

'All right, I take your point. But tell me exactly what footage you've got.'

'Well, there's you massaging Doreen – perfectly properly, of course. And you with Tanya – quite improperly, so I can hardly send that to Jeremy or anyone else.'

'Okay. Go on.'

Julia's expression grew arch. 'Oh yes, and then there's you giving a simultaneous massage to those two model girls. I don't know what you thought you were up to!'

Grant grinned wryly, wrenching her heart in the process. 'Well, I can tell you now. They begged me to fit them both into the same session, spun me some line about working next day and having no time to book separate appointments. Anyway, in return for my co-operation they promised to recruit more club members. So, being already somewhat smitten by you and hoping to get into your good books, I agreed.'

Julia laughed. 'So that's your story, is it? Well, Lou and Rebecca *did* introduce some more members, but recently they went even further and organised a petition against Cadstock. They managed to get over fifty signatures.'

'Really? That's marvellous!'

He had taken her hand quite spontaneously and, although she slowly withdrew it again, Julia felt a warm rush of pleasure at his touch. 'I'm not so sure. I've sent it on to the council, but I've a feeling that one rather high-profile MP counts for a lot more than fifty local women, however influential.'

Again Grant sank back into thought. Julia rose from the sofa, needing to be free of the turmoil his nearness aroused in her. But even at a distance he exerted a powerful pull on her body that threatened to wreck the tight resolve she'd built against him.

'Okay, so what else do you have taped?' he asked. 'Besides our own session, I mean.'

Julia felt herself blush. 'Well, there's some film of Doreen and Tanya in the sauna.'

Grant leaned forward, his eyes suddenly alert. 'What? When?'

'Oh, one time Tanya booked the sauna for her exclusive use. We allow couples to do that. It's the only time a woman can bring a man into the club. The members don't take advantage of it all that often, but . . .'

'What's on it?'

'On the video? Well, I didn't watch all of it but it was pretty obvious that they hadn't just gone in there for a chat.'

'You mean they were making love to each other?' Julia nodded. He seemed excited. So much for accusing *her* of voyeurism! 'But that's fantastic! Don't you see, Julia? That's exactly what we need!'

'No, I don't see. Not really. I don't see that it's any more useful to have lesbian goings-on in my club than heterosexual ones.'

'But the difference is, in this case you're not responsible. I mean, it's not part of the service. The fact that it takes place on your premises can hardly be seen as your responsibility. All the woman did was hire the sauna for an hour.'

'Okay. But where does that get us?'

Grant smiled. 'It could just get us out of this mess. It could just be the one usable bit of footage that we can send . . . or threaten to send . . . to Cadstock.'

She stared at him, deciding to ignore for the moment his blatant use of the words 'us' and 'we'. Maybe, just maybe, he'd hit on something.

'Okay, I'll go along with that for now. What exactly do you suggest I should do with it, then?'

'Doreen, she's the one to approach. And I think I'm the one to do it.'

'Really, Grant, don't you think you've done enough dam—'

'Hear me out, please Julia. I've got a plan. Doreen gave me a PO box number to use. In case I got hold of any hot material that I wanted to send her—'

'Grant!'

He ignored her reproving glance and continued. 'I didn't use it because things never got that far but I could make use of it now, send her a couple of stills from the video and say I'd like to talk to her about them. I'd word it so she could hardly refuse.'

'So we *are* talking blackmail!'

'If you like. But I think the situation warrants it, don't you? It's your business at stake – and my peace of mind.'

She frowned. 'How do you mean?'

Grant's face darkened. 'Julia, I have to prove to you that I'm on your side. I have to do something to help. I've hardly been able to sleep since you sacked me.'

Julia knew how he felt, but still she couldn't bring herself to say she forgave him. Deciding to shelve that painful issue, she asked him what he'd say to Doreen.

'I'm not sure, I'd have to think it through carefully. But she might be able to get Cadstock to spare *Sybarites*, and the new club. I don't know how she'd do it. Maybe she could try some blackmail of her own, involving Tanya. But I'd make it clear that if she didn't succeed that video would be sent not only to Jeremy but to the editor of the *Gazette* as well.'

Julia still looked doubtful. It seemed not only a long shot but a dangerous one, too. Yet what else was open to her? Maybe she should let Grant have this one chance to put things right.

Grant saw her hesitation. He rose and came over to her, taking her hand again, looking into her eyes with a smile that sent seductive messages quivering through all the sensory pathways of her body.

He glanced at his watch. 'Could we go over to the club now, and pick up the video? I know a place where I could get some stills done, first thing tomorrow.'

Julia hesitated. It was ten past eleven, and the club would be deserted by the time they got there. 'Well, we could. I have the keys. But . . .'

'Then let's go. The way I see it, there's no time to lose.'

She nodded, fetched her bag and slipped a jacket over her shoulders. Grant led the way downstairs and out into his waiting car. They drove to the club scarcely speaking, each lost in their own thoughts. Julia was trying not to think of this as anything more than an extension of their business relationship but it was very difficult. With Grant beside her, his clean-etched profile staring straight ahead into the night, she was tempted to talk about more intimate matters, but she knew this was not the time. If there were any post-mortem to be held about their short-lived affair it was not her place to initiate it.

Sybarites was ghostly quiet as they walked through the corridor to her office. She unlocked the inner door and searched through the videos while Grant watched.

'This is it!' she held it up. 'Want to see?'

'Can you freeze-frame it?' She nodded. 'Okay.

Start a way in and run it through slowly. I want to see if there are any suitable shots.'

The image that came up on the screen was of Tanya enthusiastically licking Doreen's pussy while she stimulated herself with her hand.

'Is that explicit enough for you?' Julia asked him wryly.

Grant stared at it with close attention. 'I should say so.'

'Find it stimulating, do you?' Julia sounded scathing.

Grant turned on her with a frown. 'Not particularly. I'm thinking of how useful it will be, that's all.'

'Oh yes. Of course!'

His blue eyes sought hers out, frank and challenging. 'Look, I know you and I have a lot of unfinished business to sort out. I really regret the way things went wrong between us, and I'm sure you do too.'

'Water under the bridge, old boy,' she said airily. But her heart ached.

'Talking of water ... would you think it very cheeky of me if I asked to use your pool?'

'What?'

'Okay, forget it!'

'No, I was just surprised, that's all. You want a swim, right now?'

'I miss working here,' he explained. 'Being able to use the facilities. I just had a sudden urge to plunge into that lovely warm water for a midnight swim.'

Julia shrugged. 'If you really want to. I'll come and unlock the pool area.'

She watched from the sidelines, averting her gaze as he stripped naked, then saw him plunge into the still water, sending blue ripples out to every corner of the pool. He swam several lengths, his strong brown arms cleaving the water like a machine. Then he stopped at the shallow end and looked up at her.

'Want to join me?'

Julia shook her head, but it was a half-hearted gesture. She realised she did want to, very much indeed. Right then there was little more inviting than that big, warm bath.

Grant smiled. 'Suit yourself!'

When he had his back to her, ploughing up the pool again, she made up her mind. Slipping quickly out of her jeans and top, she was in the water before he had turned round at the other end. When he did see her he paused, grinning, for her to catch up with him.

'Race you?' he suggested.

'No thanks, I prefer something more relaxing.'

She turned away and swam the few strokes that took her to the steps of the whirlpool. Clambering into the round basin she flicked the switch that set the water gently bubbling and settled down in it with a sigh, closing her eyes. When she opened them again, Grant had joined her.

It was as if the effervescent water had suddenly become electrically charged. Julia couldn't help remembering that last time, when she'd fantasised about Grant while letting the friction of the water jet bring her off. She realised that she didn't want him any less now. If anything her desire was stronger, knowing what incredible pleasure he was able to give her for real, not just in her dreams. He caught her looking at him through her lids and smiled.

'Julia, don't you have that *déjà vu* feeling?' She smiled at him, unable to resist those tender eyes. 'Don't you wish you could put the clock back to that last time, before everything went wrong between us?'

'Maybe . . .'

'I wish there were some way we could. I know it's not easy to learn to trust again. I've been kicking myself for not coming clean with you before, but I was so afraid of putting you off me altogether, and I wanted you so much.'

Her stomach gave a sudden lurch at the thought of him desiring her, as much as she wanted him. She sighed and began to talk, relishing the release after so many weeks of silent recriminations.

'You saw Leo, saw what he was like. My marriage to him left scars and, until you came along, I hadn't dared risk giving myself to anyone else. That weekend . . .' She faltered, as the tears of loss and disillusion threatened to fall.

'I know.' He reached out under water and squeezed her hand. 'But how many times can a man say he's sorry? I'm doing what I can to save your business. But is there any hope of saving our relationship?'

She knew he was being totally open with her, and perhaps she owed him as much in return. But still there was a hard knot of resistance in her, a wound that stubbornly refused to heal.

'I don't know, Grant,' she said miserably.

'Well, if you wanted to punish me you're doing a good job!'

Julia saw his face suddenly change as an idea hit him. He gave her a mischievous grin that baffled but also secretly delighted her.

'Julia, how about if you really vented your feelings on me, gave me what you thought I deserved?'

'What do you mean?'

'Come on!' He took her hand and led her out of the spa bath and into the main pool, where they swam a length together before getting out. Still grinning, he handed her one of the towelling robes

194

that hung on a wall hook and slipped the other one round himself.

'What is this, Grant?'

But he only smiled at her, sphinx-like, and led the way to the door. They crossed the reception area, now eerily silvered by the full moon that was peeping in through the glass of the front door, down the corridor past the Healthfood Bar to the gym.

'Got the key?'

Still mystified, Julia selected the right key from the bunch she'd put in her pocket. The gym stood dark and silent, all the machines at rest. Grant flicked on the light, still grinning, and announced, 'Welcome to the Punishment Room!'

'Grant, what are you playing at?'

'You'll see.'

Julia watched incredulously as he went over to the weights machine in the centre of the room and straddled the bench. He pulled the sash from his robe and threw it to Julia then stripped and caught hold of the iron bar dangling above his head. Pulling it down like a yoke behind his neck he knelt on all fours on the bench.

Staring uncomprehendingly at his naked back, lean thighs and taut buttocks, Julia said, 'What the hell are you doing?'

He turned his head, with difficulty, and grinned at her. 'Tie my hands to this bar.'

'Why?'

'Never mind, just do as I say.'

Shrugging, she tied the towelling belt to the bar then wound it first around one wrist then the other in a figure of eight, securing the other end with another knot. 'Is that okay?'

'Perfect.' His voice changed to a mock intoning. 'And now, O most powerful and beauteous

Mistress, I am under your yoke. You may do with me whatever you desire. If I have offended, chastise me as severely as my offence warrants and I shall accept my punishment willingly.'

Chapter Fifteen

JULIA GIGGLED. THE sight of Grant's lean buttocks rearing provocatively up at her from the bench aroused conflicting feelings. She couldn't help finding it ridiculous, yet from deep within her came a surge of the kind of excitement she felt when she was on top and in control. Running *Sybarites* frequently gave her that kind of a buzz, but never before had she felt it at this most intimate and personal level.

Grant craned his neck round behind the bar and looked up at her with a grin. 'Now it's your turn to humiliate and embarrass me,' he explained. 'I promised I shall take my punishment like a man.'

His torso was twisted round, allowing Julia to glimpse his genitals. She noticed with some interest that his penis was already stiffening, and the sight added an extra dimension to her growing excitement. 'What do you want me to do?' she asked, her voice husky.

'It's not what I want, but what you want,' Grant corrected her. 'I've put myself completely in your hands. Punish me for my misdemeanours any way you wish.'

Julia bent forward and gave him an experimental

slap on the behind. The cheeks of his buttocks felt pleasantly firm and smooth, so she smacked him again quite a bit harder, making her palm sting. I can't believe I'm doing this, she thought. Raising her right arm she brought it down with even more force, so that the sharp sound of the slap echoed round the gym and Grant let out an involuntary grunt.

Finding her robe was getting in the way, Julia slipped it off and set about the task in a more efficient way. Standing right behind him, astride the bench, she delivered a series of rhythmic blows to Grant's reddening rear end.

'Okay, this is for betraying me to that bitch Doreen!' Slap!

'And this is for breaking the rules with those model girls!' Whack!

'And here's one for making me feel jealous of that tart Tanya!' Slap!

'And now one for making me want you!' Smack!

'And another for all my sleepless nights!' Slap!

'And for confirming my suspicions that all men are bastards!' Crack!

Now Julia was really in her stride, puffing and panting with the exertion, her breasts shuddering at each blow. There was a fine film of sweat over her, and her hair was plastered down on one side of her brow. Grant's tanned behind had a rosy flush to it yet he still knelt, patient as a mule, ready for whatever else she wanted to do to him.

What Julia wanted now was closer contact. Her body ached for his, for the exquisite feel of flesh against flesh. She sank down on to the padded bench behind him and sidled forward, her open labia rubbing against the cushioning leather. Reaching round Grant's back she hugged him close, her breasts squashed against his warm, damp skin, her fingers encountering the matted hair of his chest. Grant groaned, the muscles and sinews of his shoulders still twisted as they took the strain of the punishing yoke. Her hands dropped lower, tangled in the thicker bush at the base of his stomach, felt the tall rod of flesh brush against them as Grant's erection reached its peak. Leaning her face between the jutting blades of his shoulders, Julia closed her eyes and grasped his penis with both hands, her left hand encircling the thick base and her right hand cradling the top of his shaft. He made a soft noise, halfway between a sigh and a moan.

'I'm going to make you come!' Julia whispered.

Again she felt the thrill of being in complete control. It had never occurred to her before that she could so easily have this sexual power over a man. Always she had thought of masturbating or fellating a man as a favour, something he wanted her to do and which, to some degree, demeaned her. Now she realised that it was all a question of attitude. A man aroused was at her mercy, she could satisfy him as quickly or as slowly as she wished. Or, if she really wanted to punish him, she could be a tormenting prick-tease.

But Grant had taken his punishment. All the anger that Julia had felt towards him was spent, for the time being at least. She preferred a subtler method of imposing her will on him.

Slowly Julia began to caress his rampant organ, lifting the foreskin over the glans then pulling it gently back. She could feel the urgent, pent-up energy flowing through her fingers, the desire to thrust and plunge that she was denying him. The first time he tried to push against her hand she clenched the shaft tightly, checking the movement. The second time, she reinforced her message with a sharp nip on the back of his neck, making Grant cry out. She wanted him passive beneath her fingers, his cock no longer his instrument but her plaything.

New dimensions of pleasure were opening up for Julia as she orchestrated the progress of Grant's arousal. Her tactics were infinitely varied. She ran tentative fingertips over the moistening tip then, judging him to be too wet, returned to the root of his sturdy erection and massaged it with her thumbs for a while. Sometimes she would roll the length of him between her palms, as if she were preparing clay for the kiln, or pastry for the oven. Or, finding him just a bit too flaccid, she would seize his stalk between her thumb and forefinger to give him a few seconds of vigorous rubbing until he hardened again. If she felt the blood rushing too quickly through the organ she would simply hold it gently for a while until the rush of premature excitement ceased. Then she would resume her gentle stimulation, cradling the glans within the hollow of her palm while her fingertips moved the loose skin over his shaft with soft, caressing strokes.

She heard Grant moan, 'Oh God, Julia!' and knew that the subtle torment she was inflicting on him was going to result in one of the most intense orgasms he'd ever had. But not yet. For a while she wanted to luxuriate in her own increasing arousal. Already the leather bench was wet with the juices seeping from between her swollen labia, and the soft friction of her nipples against his back was delightfully arousing. Taking one hand from the front of him she gently squeezed her left breast then quickly felt herself below.

The delicate tissues were wide open to her touch, soft and frilly, while at their heart she could feel the solid nub of her desire grown huge and sensitised, near to delivering the relief she craved. She spread her thighs wider, nudging close to Grant's buttocks, and wriggled her pelvis against him to stimulate her clitoris. In her hand his penis reared and twitched, longing for the release which she was so cruelly denying him. She sensed that he was wearying of the strain on his shoulders, too, but it was all part of his punishment.

Perhaps it was time to take pity on him. Julia began the firm, steady hand movements which she knew would soon bring him to a climax. At the same time she rubbed her mons against the taut mounds of his behind, her tumid lower lips brushing back and forth over his buttocks. It was good, but it was not good enough. Julia knew she wouldn't come that way, and now she was having a taste of her own medicine, hovering on the brink the way she had kept Grant waiting for the past twenty minutes or so.

His low, voluptuous moans were driving her wild. She buried her mouth in the sweet flesh of his neck, tasting the salt sweat as she gyrated her hips and pumped her hands, poised between her desire to make him spill his seed and her own lust for fulfilment. At last Grant's drawn-out agony ended in a series of wild spurts that flew across the gym, accompanied by deep groans that set up answering shudders in Julia's womb. Not that she was totally satisfied, but there was an emotional release, the satisfaction of having somehow proved something and, from somewhere dark inside her, a gloating sense of triumph that she had made him wait so long for it.

Seeing him slump forward Julia untied his bonds and let him rest. While he did so she went to the red rubber exercise mat in the corner and dragged it over beside the bench. Grant watched with puzzled, spent eyes as she lay down on it and spread her thighs.

'Come on!' she urged him. 'Now it's my turn!'

Wearily he staggered from his post and came to kneel beside her on the mat.

'Lick me!' she commanded him.

Obediently Grant bent his head to the task, at the same time fondling her breast with his right hand. Now he was licking her from above, the way she liked it, his wet tongue sliding easily over the already pulsating button of her clitoris, pushing her closer and closer to her goal. His other hand began dabbling in her sex, probing gently, making her clench her muscles around his fingers to intensify the sensations. She writhed and moaned softly, aware that he was doing exactly what she wanted, that she could just lie back and take her pleasure selfishly, without thought. Not even while he massaged her had she felt this self-indulgent, this free to ask of him whatever she wished. He was her sex slave, and whatever she asked of him he would carry out.

Not that she wished to test him. Julia was perfectly content with having him perform cunnilingus on her for as long as she desired. She was so sopping wet down below that it was almost impossible to distinguish between his slick tongue and her own slippery folds. The pulsating focus of her lust was now racing out of control. Feeling the swift acceleration towards a climax begin Julia gave a guttural moan and submitted to the sharp pangs of ecstasy that his expert tonguing produced. Once the series of fierce spasms had ended she commanded him to lick and suck her sensitive breasts, to keep her ticking over until she was ready to repeat the process.

Next time she had him rub her down below while he continued to mouth her rigid, elongated nipples. It didn't take long for Julia to begin the ascent towards orgasm again. Like a well-oiled machine her clitoris responded to the friction within a few minutes and her response was even more intense, the rippling fire spreading far beyond her lower region, down all the pathways of her nervous system to the very tips of her fingers and toes. The wonderful tingling lingered on after the last spasm had died away, leaving her exhausted but wholly satisfied.

Through weary, bleary eyes, Julia looked up at Grant. He was still sitting by her side, a faint smile on his handsome face, and she felt a gush of some unadmitted emotion well up in her, something she had no words for. Helplessly she watched him carry her limp hand to his lips then let it fall on the mat again. Through the confused maze that had once been her mind, Julia was dimly aware that a barrier had been breached that night. They had been acting on some more atavistic level, experiencing a primeval power trip that had been almost frightening in its intensity. What the pair of them had shared went beyond love, to some realm of the senses where psychology and physiology met in shameless accord.

Yet could she have acted that way, enjoyed exercising her power over him, if they hadn't already shared a weekend of tender and mutual love? With a shock Julia realised that, in the realm of the sexual, she still trusted Grant absolutely. He might have wronged her as an employee but as a lover he was still the best she could ever hope to have.

Smiling up at him, she was slightly disconcerted to see him spring to his feet with an air of 'job done' about him.

'Come on, Julia.' Grant held out a hand to help her up. 'Let's go and dress, then pick up that video. It's gone two and I'm shattered.'

The intrusion of his everyday tone into her ultra-mellow mood was almost more than Julia could bear, but she rose nevertheless and went to put on her robe. Grant said little as they returned to the pool, put on their clothes then went back to her office. Trying to ignore the growing void inside her, Julia locked up after them then followed him out to his car. He would have to drive her home. Surely he would stay the night?

But he didn't. Grant dropped her at her door, promised to give her a ring as soon as there were any developments, then bade her a curt goodnight before driving off into the night. Wearily Julia climbed up to her flat, stripped off and fell into bed. It was hard to believe that he could be so cool with her, after what they'd been through. Had she done or said something wrong? Tormenting herself with an action replay of the night's events Julia stayed awake until dawn then finally drifted off into an uneasy slumber.

For a week Julia heard nothing more from Grant. After the sexually-charged high of their encounter in the gym, she almost sank back into self-doubt, but something stopped her from being over-whelmed by such negative emotion. There was a sense of completeness inside her, such as she'd never known before, and the feeling that she and Grant had somehow wiped the slate clean.

Somehow Julia managed to summon up the confidence to press forward with her new business venture. By Friday afternoon she had ordered the demolition men to start work the following Monday, and her discussions with the builders were well under way. All being well, work would start on the holistic health centre in ten days' time.

All being well. The spectre of Jeremy Cadstock continued to haunt Julia in odd moments, and despite her show of optimism her faith in Grant's plan of action was slim. Her licence came up for renewal at the end of the month and by starting work on the new building before then she was taking a gamble. She reflected ironically that Leo, who had always sneered at her for being too timid to take risks, would have been amazed by her foolhardiness.

Then, almost as soon as she returned home that evening, there was a call from Grant. His tone was urgent.

'Julia, there's been an extraordinary development and I must talk to you about it. Can I come round?'

Julia's heart was beating rapidly at the thought of seeing him again. She was also eaten up with curiosity. 'Right now?'

'If that's convenient.'

'Sure. Have you eaten? I was just going to cook some pasta.'

'Great! See you in about twenty minutes.'

While she defrosted a home-made sauce, Julia had a quick shower and changed into a mulberry silk shirt and navy leggings. She wore little make-up and let her hair fall naturally to her shoulders, but splashed on some perfume. Her desire for Grant was growing every second, and she was praying that he would be feeling the same.

The moment Grant appeared his eyes said it all. He wanted her. For a few seconds Julia luxuriated in the thought that they might just end up in bed together that evening.

First, though, there was something he had to tell her, something extraordinary. Scarcely waiting for her to finish pouring him a drink he began, 'Julia, you'll never guess. Tanya's pregnant!'

'What?'

'It's true, and it's Cadstock's. Doreen told me. I sent her those lesbian photos with a cryptic note and she agreed to meet me. Apparently she thought

I was trying to warn her, that I was still on her side. But she said there was no need to worry because her husband's mistress would soon be out of the running. I asked her what she meant, and she told me straight. That's the reason Tanya's disappeared off the scene. She wanted to have the child and bring it up as a single mother, with no publicity. Some hope!'

Julia sat down on the sofa beside him with a thud. 'I can't believe it! Are you quite sure?'

'Doreen was the first person Tanya confided in. They're supposed to be friends, remember? Or *were* friends. Jeremy doesn't know yet, but he will tomorrow. It'll be plastered all over the front pages of the nationals.'

'How did they find out?'

'I reckon Doreen tipped them off. Anonymously, probably. So we've all got what we want without any more dirty dealings. Tanya's got Jeremy's baby, Doreen's got hubby back and the Clean-Up Campaign will have lost all credibility. The only loser in all of this is Cadstock himself and, quite frankly, he deserves it. The best he can expect now is a return to back-bench obscurity and the hope of keeping his seat at the next election.'

Julia smiled, feeling herself suddenly freed from the grey cloud that had been hovering about her for weeks. She lifted her sherry glass.

'Here's to *Sybarites*, and the new centre!'

Grant nodded, but his blue eyes had an unspoken question lurking in them.

Julia added, 'I'm very grateful to you for doing what you could to help, Grant.'

He shrugged. 'Does that mean we're quits now?'

'If you like.'

'But I suppose it's too much to ask if I can have my old job back?'

206

Julia hesitated. Did he know how much she wanted him, and in how many ways? His gaze burned into hers, trying to read her mind. His guard was down, letting her read his, and she knew that he would give anything to be close to her again.

Mischievously she shook her head. 'No, Grant, I'm sorry. That's impossible. I've already hired a replacement for you.'

'I see.' She perversely enjoyed seeing the way his shoulders slumped with disappointment, his mouth turned down at the corners.

He gave a sigh. 'Well, maybe I'll take up your ex-husband's offer of a croupier job. After all, his business interests should be safe now, too.'

Julia put down her glass then took Grant's out of his hand and set it down on the coffee table beside hers. Turning round, she faced him squarely.

'It's up to you, of course. But I do have something else to offer you, or have you forgotten?'

'Forgotten?'

'That I offered to make you manager of the new club.'

'Yes, I know. But . . .'

'The offer still stands, Grant. If you feel you could handle it.'

She saw his eyes reflecting the almost imperceptible moment when the skies turn from grey to blue. 'Are you sure?' he said incredulously.

Julia nodded. 'If we can both forgive and forget.'

'There's nothing to forgive,' he said simply. 'On my side, at least. I regret saying certain things to you, but I hope you think I've been punished enough.'

Julia raised one quizzical brow. 'Oh, I don't know about that! But maybe it's me who should have been punished. After all, I didn't trust you enough to believe your story. That's what I regret.'

His response was swift and, in the circumstances, predictable. Leaning across the brief space between them he caught her in his arms and gave her a crushing kiss that set her senses reeling. Soon his mouth was travelling down her neck, seeking the hollow at the base of her throat, leaving a trail of fire. Julia felt him undo the top three buttons of her shirt so that his questing tongue could enter the deep ravine of her cleavage, making her gasp with the sheer delight of having him make love to her again.

'Grant . . . shall we go to the bedroom?' she murmured, eager for the freedom of nakedness and the space of her comfortable large bed.

'I think so, don't you?'

He smiled down at her ironically as he rose from the sofa then scooped her up into his arms. She let him take her through, gazing up at him like a love-struck teenager all the while, until he deposited her gently on the bed. After first easing her out of her shirt, then her leggings, he stood back and appraised her body in its black silk underwear. Julia felt her skin respond to the lustful caress of his sapphire eyes, every inch of her subtly vibrating with longing and expectation. She watched him take off his shirt to expose the brown, sculpted chest, then he unbuckled his belt, a mysterious smile on his face. He came towards the bed, still smiling, holding the belt in both hands.

'I let you escape me once,' he said. 'But it won't happen again. Especially not tonight.'

Before she understood the true meaning of his words Grant had put her wrists together above her head and swiftly bound them with his belt. For an instant Julia felt a frisson of fear. Had he been lying to her about forgiving and forgetting? Did he still harbour a grudge? Was he about to exact some painful revenge for the thrashing she'd given him the other night? She could feel her heart thudding anxiously as he knelt on the bed beside her, studying her face.

Then he whispered, 'Trust me, Julia,' and she understood.

Already published

BACK IN CHARGE
Mariah Greene

A woman in control. Sexy, successful, sure of herself and of what she wants, Andrea King is an ambitious account handler in a top advertising agency. Life seems sweet, as she heads for promotion and enjoys the attentions of her virile young boyfriend.

But strange things are afoot at the agency. A shake-up is ordered, with the key job of Creative Director in the balance. Andrea has her rivals for the post, but when the chance of winning a major new account presents itself, she will go to any lengths to please her client – and herself . . .

0 7515 1276 1

THE DISCIPLINE OF PEARLS
Susan Swann

A mysterious gift, handed to her by a dark and arrogant stranger. Who was he? How did he know so much about her? How did he know her life was crying out for something different? Something . . . exciting, erotic?

The pearl pendant, and the accompanying card bearing an unknown telephone number, propel Marika into a world of uninhibited sexuality, filled with the promise of a desire she had never thought possible. The Discipline of Pearls . . . an exclusive society that speaks to the very core of her sexual being, bringing with it calls to ecstasies she is powerless to ignore, unwilling to resist . . .

0 7515 1277 X

HOTEL APHRODISIA
Dorothy Starr

The luxury hotel of Bouvier Manor nestles near a spring whose mineral water is reputed to have powerful aphrodisiac qualities. Whether this is true of not, Dani Stratton, the hotel's feisty receptionist, finds concentrating on work rather tricky, particularly when the muscularly attractive Mitch is around.

And even as a mysterious consortium threatens to take over the Manor, staff and guests seem quite unable to control their insatiable thirsts . . .

0 7515 1287 7

AROUSING ANNA
Nina Sheridan

Anna had always assumed she was frigid. At least, that's what her husband Paul had always told her – in between telling her to keep still during their weekly fumblings under the covers and playing the field himself during his many business trips.

But one such trip provides the chance that Anna didn't even know she was yearning for. Agreeing to put up a lecturer who is visiting the university where she works, she expects to be host to a dry, elderly academic, and certainly isn't expecting a dashing young Frenchman who immediately speaks to her innermost desires. And, much to her delight and surprise, the vibrant Dominic proves himself able and willing to apply himself to the task of arousing Anna . . .

0 7515 1222 2

PLAYING THE GAME
Selina Seymour

Kate has had enough. No longer is she prepared to pander to the whims of lovers who don't love her; no longer will she cater for their desires while neglecting her own.

But in reaching this decision Kate makes a startling discovery: the potency of her sexual urge, now given free rein through her willingness to play men at their own game. And it is an urge that doesn't go unnoticed – whether at her chauvinistic City firm, at the château of a new French client, or in performing the duties of a high-class call girl . . .

0 7515 1189 7

Forthcoming publications

SATURNALIA
Zara Devereux

Recently widowed, Heather Logan is concerned about her sex-life. Even when married it was plainly unsatisfactory, and now the prospects for sexual fulfilment look decidedly thin.

After consulting a worldly friend, however, Heather takes his advice and checks in to Tostavyn Grange, a private hotel-cum-therapy centre for sexual inhibition. Heather had been warned about their 'unconventional' methods, but after the preliminary session, in which she is brought to a thunderous climax – her first – she is more than willing to complete the course . . .

0 7515 1342 3

DARES
Roxanne Morgan

It began over lunch. Three different women, best friends, decide to spice up their love-lives with a little extra-curricular sex. Shannon is first, accepting the dare of seducing a motorcycle despatch rider – while riding pillion through the streets of London.

The others follow, Nadia and Corey, hesitant at first but soon willing to risk all in the pursuit of new experiences and the heady thrill of trying to out-do each other's increasingly outrageous dares . . .

0 7515 1341 5

[ ]	Back in Charge	Mariah Greene	£4.99
[ ]	The Discipline of Pearls	Susan Swann	£4.99
[ ]	Hotel Aphrodisia	Dorothy Star	£4.99
[ ]	Arousing Anna	Nina Sheridan	£4.99
[ ]	Playing the Game	Selina Seymour	£4.99

X Libris offers an eXciting range of quality titles which can be ordered from the following address:

Little, Brown and Company (UK),
P.O. Box 11,
Falmouth,
Cornwall TR10 9EN

Alternatively you may fax your order to the above address.
FAX No. 0326 376423.

Payments can be made as follows: cheque, postal order (payable to Little, Brown and Company) or by credit cards, Visa/Access. Do not send cash or currency. UK customers and B.F.P.O. please allow £1.00 for postage and packing for the first book, plus 50p for the second book, plus 30p for each additional book up to a maximum charge of £3.00 (7 books plus).

Overseas customers including Ireland please allow £2.00 for the first book plus £1.00 for the second book, plus 50p for each additional book.

NAME (Block Letters) _____

_____

ADDRESS _____

_____

_____

☐ I enclose my remittance for _____

☐ I wish to pay by Access/Visa card

Number _____

Card Expiry Date _____